The Christmas Star

"Ace Collins has been a popular author for a long time, with good reason. His Christmas series of nonfiction books combines fascinating information with inspirational story-telling; his novels make for compelling reading. In this new novel, Ace Collins combines the best of both genres and adds a realistic small-town atmosphere set during the first Christmas after World War II ends. He brings a powerful lesson about a quiet life well lived, choices that can permanently alter the course of one's life, and the grace of God, which can overcome all obstacles."
—Dave "Doc" Kirby, Host of "On the Bookshelf" and "Book Bits" (WTBF-AM/FM Troy, Ala.; CCFS Cape Town, South Africa)

"The master of Christmas nonfiction has brought us a gem of a Christmas novel. Few know Christmas like Ace Collins, and he has woven together an uplifting story perfect for the season."
—Jeffrey D. Root, Dean, School of Humanites, Ouachita Baptist University

THE CHRISTMAS STAR

Ace Collins

Abingdon Press fiction
a novel approach to faith

Nashville, Tennessee

The Christmas Star

Copyright © 2012 by Ace Collins

ISBN-13: 978-1-4267-1468-9

Published by Abingdon Press, P.O. Box 801, Nashville, TN 37202

www.abingdonpress.com

Library of Congress Cataloging-in-Publication Data

Collins, Ace.
  The Christmas star / Ace Collins.
    p. cm.
  ISBN 978-1-4267-1468-9 (book - pbk. / trade pbk. : alk. paper) 1. Christmas stories.
2. Medal of Honor—Fiction. I. Title.
  PS3553.O47475C47 2012
  813'.54—dc23

2012028330

Printed in the United States of America

1 2 3 4 5 6 7 8 9 10 / 17 16 15 14 13 12

To the community that is Ouachita!

Acknowledgments

No book is created in a vacuum, and I'd like to thank the following people for all their assistance: John Hillman, Joyce Hart, Ramona Richards, Susan Cornell, and Teri Wilhelms.

1

———∞∞∞———

December 21, 1945, 3:20 p.m.

Sharp County had never experienced such a collective sense of euphoria. First, the Great Depression and then the war had created an atmosphere of heartache, insecurity, chaos, and turmoil, tearing up families while dashing dreams and crushing security. Now there was a hope fueled by the fact that freedom had been preserved, and "Peace on Earth" was no longer just a line on a greeting card; it was a reality. Christmas was more than just a holiday this year; it was a celebration! The promise that had been offered in Bing Crosby's hit single "I'll Be Home for Christmas" had been realized and for almost everyone in every corner of this part of Arkansas, as well as all over the United States, it was the most wonderful time of the year, the decade, and perhaps even the century.

December 21 was the day everyone in the rural school district, children and teachers alike, had been looking forward to. For those spending seven hours a day behind the native stone walls of Ash Flat High, 3:20 p.m. was the moment when Christmas really began. As the clock signaled that specific instant and the final bell sounded, kids poured through the

———∞∞∞———

old two-story school building's large oak front door and down the well-worn concrete steps like the bulls racing through the streets of Pamplona, Spain. Their warm spirits met a cold north wind as scores of enthusiastic kids rushed across the yard and onto Calvin Jenkins' yellow GMC school bus. Other equally ecstatic youngsters raced past the mud-splattered vehicle, up the dirt road toward downtown Ash Flat, just to spy all the wonder that was waiting to be discovered in the community's handful of stores. Smiles and laughter were everywhere, as everyone seemed caught up in holiday spirit—everyone but Jimmy Reed.

While others rushed past at supersonic speed, Jimmy, a tall, thin sixteen-year-old, hung back at the top of the steps, a tormented look filling his deep green eyes. Dressed in a blue wool jacket that was about two sizes too small, he stuck his ungloved hands deep into the pockets of his patched jeans. In a sense, he was an outcast in a world of holiday cheer. For the boy, there was no light at Christmas, only foreboding darkness brought on by great loss. While all his friends saw Christmas as a joyous dream, to Jimmy it was a nightmare, a prison of loneliness and a day of despair. If Jimmy could erase any day from the calendar, it would be December 25.

"See you in January," Wylie Rhoads called out from behind as Jimmy slowly ambled down the steps. Glancing back over his shoulder at the short, stocky school superintendent standing in the arched entry, the youth shrugged his shoulders and smirked. That expression brought an immediate response.

"Jimmy!"

"Yeah," the boy shot back at the school administrator, his voice and body language showing great contempt and little respect.

As their eyes met, the man pointed his finger and barked, "Get the chip off your shoulder, son. You've got two weeks to shape up that attitude. When you come back, I want to see a different person. Someone with the kind of character your father had."

"You leave my dad out of this," Jimmy hissed.

Marching down the steps until he was face-to-face with the angry kid, Rhoads emphasized his threats in a firm, deliberate tone. "I can't do anything about what happened to your father and neither can you. But you're driving your mom to an early grave while you're setting yourself up to end up in reform school or worse. You've got too much potential to waste it!"

"I haven't done nothing that bad," the boy snapped, his green eyes never leaving the man's.

"Not yet," Rhoads shot back. "But it's coming. I've seen it before. Starts with stuff like breaking windows, sneaking behind the fence to smoke, and going out getting drunk, but it always ends with a whole lot more. And you're heading that way at a breakneck pace."

Jimmy shook his head, "You don't know nothing."

Frustrated, Rhoads turned his back on the boy and marched back up the five steps and into the building. As he did, Jimmy leaned against the school wall and pulled a cigarette from his pocket. Who cared what old Wylie thought? So what if he got kicked out of school? It was a waste of time anyway.

"James Reed, don't you light that up on campus or anywhere else."

Audrey Lankins was one of the few students who hadn't given up on him. Like Jimmy, she was a junior, but while he had developed a knack for getting into trouble, she walked on the right side of the street. She was Ash Flat's prize student, and with her blonde hair, blue eyes, and striking figure, she was also the prettiest girl in the county as well as the youth leader at the Methodist Church. She was the ideal daughter for her banker father and the apple of everyone's eye. And as much as he didn't want to admit it, Audrey was also the one person he truly wanted to impress. Yet she couldn't know that, not now or ever. So though he yearned to reach out to her, he delivered his reply in a machine-gun fashion he hoped would shut her up and drive her away. At this point, he couldn't afford to have anyone close enough to know what he was planning.

"What do you care? You won't get in trouble if I have a smoke."

"I just care," the pretty blonde assured him. "I don't want you in trouble. That's not who you really are. You've always been my best friend, or at least that's how it used to be."

Forcing his attention toward the street, he twirled the cigarette from finger to finger of his right hand, slipping it between one and then the next with the dexterity of a magician, before finally letting it slide into his palm and easing it into his coat pocket. When the thirty-second show was over, he looked back at the girl. "Didn't feel like smoking anyway. I'll save it. But it has nothing to do with what you want. You understand?"

Audrey smiled. Clutching her black purse to her chest, she moved to the boy's side. "You coming to the church program on Sunday night?"

"Naw, got better things to do. Got something really special planned."

"I'm going to sing," she added enticingly, now she was more begging than just giving him information on the program. He approved of her approach, but he still couldn't go. There was something far more important calling him.

"And you'll do great," he mumbled, "but, like I said, there are things I got to do."

"Fine," she replied in a huff. Then, her tone changing, she added, "But it would mean a lot to me if you'd come. So please try."

He didn't understand why she cared about him, why she continued to reach out to him. Maybe it was true that good girls liked bad boys. Who knew? So, though he had no intention of stepping into her church or any other on Sunday night or on any other day, he nodded.

"Jimmy," Audrey's sweet voice pulled his eyes back to hers, "even if you don't come, you have a merry Christmas."

Shaking his head, Jimmy laughed. "Christmas is for kids. I don't need it and don't like it. I don't care if it ever comes. Just another day and not a very good one either!"

The smile drained from her face as quickly as a solitary raindrop evaporated in the scorching August sun. Pushing her hair over the shoulders of her coat, she said, "I don't understand. Everyone likes Christmas, and on top of that everyone is home this year." The words hovered in the cool air like a dark cloud. She probably knew the moment she spoke them she'd opened a wound too painful to contemplate, much less talk about. Yet words can't be unspoken, and they rarely disappear as quickly as they are said. And so her words hovered just out of her reach for moments too long to count.

Turning his face back toward the old school bus, Jimmy chewed on Audrey's observation. She'd opened a large door to a place where no one would have thought him rude to lash out at the girl. If the superintendent, or a teacher, or even one of his friends had spit out what she'd just said, he'd have jumped on them. But this was Audrey; she was incapable of pouring salt in a wound. It wasn't her nature. So, after taking a deep breath, he said, "Christmas was OK when I was a kid, but that was before the war."

Moving two steps closer, Audrey placed her right hand delicately on his shoulder and whispered, "What I said was stupid. I'm sorry."

"Nothing to be sorry for," he mumbled, once more digging his hands deeply into his pockets. After all, she was not the one who had changed everything. She had no part in it. Christmas had once been wonderful for him, too. There were still bittersweet memories that were woven into the fabric of his mind. He and his father had always gone out into the woods to find and cut a tree, drag it into the house, and laugh about a host of different things. And they had strung popcorn while Jimmy's mother pulled out old decorations and hung them on the tree.

After their turkey dinner and a dessert of homemade pecan pie, his dad would pull out his Gibson guitar, and for more than an hour they would sing every carol they knew, many three and four times. And they always ended with "Silent Night," with his dad explaining the story behind the song before they sang all the verses. Finally, just before bed, Jimmy's mother picked up his father's well-worn Bible and read from Luke about Jesus' birth while Jimmy moved the pieces of their hand-carved nativity scene across the coffee table to match her words.

But the war had changed most of that. Yes, the nativity scene was still on the table. Yes, they still cut and decorated the tree. But now the Gibson remained propped against the wall, as did the innocent joy that had once defined those December days. And it wasn't just Christmas the war had changed, though the wounds might hurt the worst on December 25; in truth the war had altered everything.

"Jimmy," Audrey's voice brought him back from the past to 1945. "You OK?"

"Yeah," he said, straightening his shoulders and forcing a smile.

"Your dad," she said, her hand still lingering on his shoulder, her light touch pushing through the coat and into his heart, "was a great man."

It was funny, Jimmy had once used those same words to describe Robert Reed. He'd boasted to his friends, including Audrey, that his father would lick the Japs all by himself. Back then, he supported that bragging by quoting from long, hand-written letters he and his mother had received from the Pacific Front. When he told what was in those communications, his friends hovered around Jimmy at the lunch table, completely awed by the fact that a Marine from their small town was fighting the Japanese in places they'd never heard of.

But all the bragging abruptly stopped in May 1942. Jimmy had just gotten home from school and was headed out to gather the eggs when he saw the dusty black truck pull into their long dirt lane. An old man he'd never seen, dressed in a dark blue uniform, got out of the vehicle and marched past Jimmy without saying a word or even acknowledging his existence. The stranger paused for a moment at the base of the porch, taking off his hat and smoothing his gray hair, then slowly, as if he were carrying a backbreaking load, climbed the three steps to the landing. After taking a deep breath, he knocked lightly on the weathered front door.

A few moments later, Jimmy's mother, dressed in a blue flower print dress half-covered by a yellow apron, appeared. It seemed strange to Jimmy that she said nothing and didn't even smile; rather, she simply stepped out and nodded as if she knew what the visitor wanted. He didn't speak either. Instead, he just pushed a shaky hand clutching a light brown envelope toward her. That simple action was just like turning the sound knob down on a radio; everything was suddenly tomb quiet. Marge Reed studied that envelope for almost thirty seconds, then, after wiping her hands on her apron, finally took it. No, now as he recalled those moments, Jimmy realized she really didn't take it; it was more as if she accepted it because she knew she had no choice.

Jimmy stood mute and confused as his mother pushed her auburn hair back off her forehead and took a seat in the porch swing. She stared off toward the pond for several minutes, long enough for the Western Union representative to start his old Ford truck and head back down the Reeds' quarter-mile lane to U.S. Highway 62. Only after the vehicle had disappeared over the hill in the direction of Agnos did Marge finally take a deep breath and gently tear open the communication. The thirty-eight-year-old woman studied the message on the yellow paper briefly before setting it carefully down on the swing. Showing no emotion, she resolutely pulled herself to her feet and silently walked back through the front door, closing it gently behind her.

When Jimmy heard her rattling the pots on the stove, he slipped from the yard, climbed up onto the porch, and moved quietly over to the swing. Picking up the telegram, he glanced at the message. It began simply enough, "We regret to inform you . . ."

Those words were all that was needed for an adult to know how the story ended, but it was not enough for a thirteen-year-old boy. So he read on, ". . . that Private Robert J. Reed was killed in action while fighting in the Philippines."

Jimmy read no more before dropping the telegram onto the porch's wooden planks and racing off into the woods. He would stay there, tears burning his eyes and streaming down his face, until the sun went down, and he came home a much different person than he had been just hours before.

That news changed everything. From that day forward there would be no more letters from overseas and there was suddenly no pride in being the son of a Marine. The news of the war, which had once drawn him like a moth to a flame, was now avoided.

In June 1942, his mother got a job in town at Miller's Store. Soon after that, the farm animals were sold and the fields leased to a neighbor. Yet those actions, while putting food on the table, didn't ease the pain. It was still there in October. That's when Jimmy found out his father really *was* a hero. It seemed Robert Reed had refused to retreat from his position, as others fled in the face of overwhelming odds, and instead had stubbornly manned a machine gun, holding off the advance of scores of enemy soldiers while hundreds of American Marines escaped to safety. Yet, even as others patted Jimmy on the back and spoke glowingly of the lives his father had saved, Jimmy did not care about those who had survived: his thoughts were only of the one who hadn't.

It was December 24, 1942; just at the moment his mother was placing dinner on their table, a knock at the door brought the news that would forever cast a cloud over Christmas. Three men, two Marines and one local congressman, explained that for his heroic actions Robert Reed had been awarded the Congressional Medal of Honor. With a sense of solemn pride, they handed the citation and medal to the small woman who now carried the burden of being both a mother and a father. And that was where the most painful holiday tradition began. With the trio of visitors looking on, Marge removed the yellow glass star that had always been placed atop the Christmas tree, setting it on an end table, then pulled the medal from its case and carefully draped it over the top of the old tree's highest branches. With tears in her eyes she stepped back and studied that shiny star and blue ribbon.

Tears also rushed into Jimmy's eyes. Yet his tears were not fueled by pride, they were inspired by anger. To him this star was not about heroism, it was a symbol of loss—his personal loss. And that is when the attitude took root. That is when he began to lash out. As the years passed, he embraced the attitude he saw in gangster movies—grab what you want and walk over anyone to get it. The change affected every facet of his life. He had no use for anyone in a position of authority. He didn't care about his studies. He lived to push the limits and test the rules. Life was short, his dad proved that, so he vowed to live hard and fast.

"Jimmy," Audrey looked at him with her big, sympathetic eyes.

"Got to go," he sighed.

Pushing himself off the wall, he walked toward the old yellow bus. As several little children sang "Jingle Bells" and a host of his friends talked about what they would be doing the next few days, Jimmy Reed was consumed by the hate he felt for this holiday and the star that would soon be placed on their tree. It was time to get even with Christmas, and he knew just how he was going to do it.

2

December 21, 1945, 3:35 p.m.

Jimmy guessed that Calvin Jenkins was in his late fifties. He was just over five and half feet tall. Calvin was thin and balding, crows' feet were heavily etched along the outside of his brown eyes, and deep lines ran across his broad forehead. In a world filled with impressive, powerful men just returning from the front lines, he stood out for being just the opposite. Yet though he had no obvious reason to be, Calvin was still an optimist whose voice smiled even more than his lips. Part of that optimism could be seen in the fact he'd been trying to carve a meager living off hopelessly poor and rocky soil for more than twenty-five years. The joke was that he'd been so successful at agriculture he'd been forced to take two other jobs just to make ends meet. The first was at the sale barn, where he helped Owen Gentry get ready for the weekly livestock auctions. The other was driving a bus for the local school district. Even with this additional income, he could barely keep the farm solvent. Alone, poor, and homely, and in scores of other ways too numerous to mention—to Jimmy—Calvin defined what the world would call a loser. If he'd been a fish, and a fisherman caught him, he'd have likely been thrown back.

As Jimmy stepped onto the old Chevy bus for that final ride of the year, the only seat open was right behind the driver. It was the last place Jimmy wanted to sit. By taking it, he knew that for the next thirty minutes, as the old yellow crate bounced along rocky dirt roads, he would have to listen to Calvin's constant chatter about everything from the weather to local sports. Worst of all, the man, as he endlessly droned, would pose questions that demanded answers. And Jimmy got more than enough of that line of talk at school.

"Gonna be a great Christmas," Calvin all but giggled as the bus pulled out of the city limits. "Yep, gonna be the best Christmas we've had around here since they carved Sharp County out of Lawrence County. And that's been like ninety years."

Even as he felt Calvin's eyes lock on him through the bus's rearview mirror, Jimmy said nothing. Yet pretending he didn't hear wasn't going to work for long and he knew it. Like it or not, he would be drawn into a conversation. So he was not surprised when a few seconds later came the driver's predictable first question, which demanded a reply.

"You got your shopping done?"

Shaking his head, Jimmy mumbled, "No. But it'll be easy. Only have one gift to get, that's for Mom and, as I've got no money, that narrows the choices."

Calvin nodded, "Best gifts are those that are made. That's what I've always said. People hang onto those. You just need to make her something."

"Yeah, maybe," Jimmy replied, turning his gaze to the bare hardwood trees along the Strawberry River.

"Try making an ornament for the tree," Calvin suggested. "You're pretty good with a knife. I've seen that for myself. I've heard you blow on those hickory whistles you whittled up. Carve a star or something out of a chunk of oak or walnut."

Jimmy shook his head and answered in a monotone, fully displaying his lack of enthusiasm for the direction of this discourse, "We got a star, and Mom wouldn't replace it for anything. I'll figure out something."

"Bet you will!"

After wrestling the bus around a steep curve, the driver continued his line of holiday thoughts. "Yep, Christmas is going to be special. The boys are home. No more fighting. Never seen so much joy around here. It's like a family reunion that just won't end."

"Not at our house," Jimmy shot back, his tone now laced with a combination of regret and anger.

Calvin glanced back in the mirror and nodded. He paused for a moment, as if gathering and organizing his thoughts, then added, "You gave up a lot, I'm sure that hurts. But your dad was a hero, and that's what heroes do: they lay down their lives for others. It was that way when he was alive too. Did I ever tell you about the time I got hurt and couldn't work my fields?"

Jimmy shook his head. Calvin hadn't told him about that, and he didn't want to hear the story either. But he was going to; there was no doubt about it.

"Yep, had a mule kick me so hard it broke my leg in two places," the driver explained, rubbing a spot just below his right knee. "Your mom was expecting you at the time. Boy, that has been a long time ago. A lot of water under the bridge, too, since those days! Anyway, the Depression was hitting us like a Joe Lewis left hook, and I had a mortgage on the place. I just knew I was going to lose it to the bank. But after working all day in his fields, your dad came over and worked my place. He did that for six weeks while I was laid up. I imagine he was putting in sixteen hours a day and more. You know, he wouldn't take a dime for it. Yeah, I'd have lost everything if it hadn't been for him."

Jimmy nodded. From what little he could remember, that was the way his father was. He was often so busy helping others he seemed to forget he had a son and wife at home. Jimmy recalled more than a few arguments between his parents that sprang from just that issue.

"Jimmy," Calvin continued as he pulled to a stop in front of Clyde Wiles's home. He jerked open the door and watched three energetic grade-school kids make their way down the aisle and off the bus before continuing. "There's another story you probably haven't heard either. Did you know I was married once?"

This was news! Jimmy had always assumed that the short, plain man was a confirmed bachelor. Who in their right mind would marry Calvin? The fact someone had was a story worth hearing, and so Jimmy leaned closer to the driver.

After waving at Hannah Wiles, Calvin shoved the old vehicle into first, released the clutch, and rocked the bus down the old rock road. He shifted through second and then third before picking up his story. "You were just a little guy when it all happened. Gosh, I was a happy man back then. In my eyes, Bess was the most beautiful girl this side of Batesville. Of course, love makes you look at things through rose-colored glasses. Guess, when I think about it now, she was likely as plain as I am. But even if she never won a single beauty pageant, her heart was a thing to behold. It gushed love like a freshwater spring. And her smile, well, it was like sunshine breaking through the clouds after a winter storm. It just warmed you to the core."

With no warning, Calvin eased the bus to a stop in front of Ella and Drew Richards's tiny farmhouse. Shoving the vehicle into neutral and setting the emergency brake, he got up from his seat, grabbed a cardboard box that had been sitting in the seat beside Jimmy and ambled toward the weather-beaten home. He knocked on the door, greeted the small man who answered, handed him the box, and then quickly turned and headed back to the bus. A few seconds later, he was once more in his seat and the bus was moving.

As long as he'd been riding Calvin's bus, there had been stops like this. No one had ever asked the reason why or even talked about it. The fact the driver stopped and delivered things to folks who didn't have kids was just accepted.

"Where was I?" Calvin asked as he pushed the bus up to twenty miles an hour. "Oh, yeah, I was talking about Bess and me.

"We had a great marriage for almost ten years. Didn't have any kids though. By that time, we figured we never would. Ah, but then a miracle happened. Such joy filled our house as we looked forward to the big event. Such great joy!"

The driver paused for a moment, and as he did, the smile on his pie-shaped face faded as quickly as the sunlight on a December afternoon. It was replaced with a grimace so pronounced it spread above the man's brow and onto his balding head. As he picked up his tale, his tone was as tinny as a banjo string.

"Then Bess died in childbirth. Baby did, too. She was here one day and gone the next." Calvin glanced back into the mirror and studied the boy. As he did, Jimmy thought he saw tears in those suddenly tired cow-brown eyes.

"It was the week before Christmas in 1933," Calvin explained, a catch in his voice, "I was so ready for the holidays that year. The thing I remember the most is building the baby's cradle myself. It was something, too. It was made out of tiger oak, and I'd cut the tree myself. I'd carved little animals into the top rail and stained it so pretty. Bess made a blue quilt to go in it, and we placed it by our bed. With the wood I had left over, I spent a few months carving a nativity scene to put on the table in our living room. It was to be our first Christmas tradition, and it was meant to last forever."

He paused, lifted his right hand, and wiped a bit of moisture from his cheek. As his fingers again wrapped around the steering wheel, he glanced back at Jimmy in the mirror. He swallowed hard before whispering, "And then Bess just died."

The driver took a deep breath in an effort to regain his composure. It must not have worked because it was eight more miles and seven more stops before he spoke again. By now, the bus was almost empty, just a handful of kids remaining in their seats, and the noises that had echoed off the metal walls were all but gone. When Calvin finally regained his voice, it was strong once more.

"Though he was married and had you, your dad was just a kid in my eyes. But on that day when I lost just about everything I cared about, he became a man. He worked all night making the two coffins for Bess and little Ben. They didn't look like thrown-together boxes either. They were beautiful, just as impressive as anything you'd see at a big city funeral parlor. He dug the graves too. He wouldn't let me pay him. He wouldn't hear of it. So, as I wasn't going to be needing it for my family's traditions, I gave him the nativity scene I had carved. I don't know if you ever saw it or not, but if you still have it, just remember it was my way of thanking your dad. It was hardly enough. In fact it didn't begin to cover the debt."

So that was where it came from! Those wooden figures that he'd moved when his mother read the Christmas story had been a gift for building coffins and digging graves. That was almost beyond comprehension. Just like it was unbelievable that a jolly man like Calvin had ever known great love or tragic loss. So how, after everything he'd been through, could he still seemingly embrace Christmas with such joy and grace?

"This is your stop," the driver almost hollered, easing the bus to a stop in front of the Reeds' long lane. As Jimmy got up and walked down the three steps to the door, Calvin yelled, "Ho, ho, ho, you have a Merry Christmas."

Turning, Jimmy studied the man. As their eyes met, the boy posed a question, "What do you do on Christmas?"

Calvin shrugged, "I go home, turn on the radio, and listen to music, and I kind of think about what could have been."

"Aren't you angry?" Jimmy demanded.

"What good would that do?" Calvin explained softly, "Anger is a wound that only makes things worse."

As Jimmy stepped through the open door to the ground, Calvin's voice caused him to turn back toward the bus. "Jimmy, Christmas might be about a birth, but we likely wouldn't celebrate it at all if the baby who was born in that stable hadn't done the same thing your dad did."

The confused expression painted on Jimmy's face clearly showed he wasn't following the driver's line of thought.

"Jesus giving his life for us is what made his birth important. So it is the way things ended at Easter that gives Christmas its reason for joy. Whenever I think of your dad, I think of John 15:13. If you don't know the verse, you need to read it sometime. Just remember, it's not just about dying for others in a war, it's about living for them in life too. I didn't give your dad a medal for his actions when he saved me a couple of times, but I should have."

The boy said nothing as he turned and began the trek down the lane. Maybe that was the way Calvin justified his loss, but for Jimmy connecting Jesus to his father was too long a stretch. So, there was no reason to rush home and look up that Scripture. Death was death, and the lesson it taught was that life was short and a person had to grab what he could as fast as he could to make living worthwhile. Jimmy knew his chance to grab something special was just around the corner, and if everything worked out, Christmas might just be worth remembering this year.

3

December 21, 1945, 4:15 p.m.

S he was dog-tired, as the locals said. Marge Reed had been walking the floors at Miller's Store for eight hours with only a fifteen-minute break for lunch. Maybe it was the fact the war was over and the troops were home or maybe it was the uptick in the economy, but for the past week they had been nearly overwhelmed with shoppers. And they weren't just looking, they were buying, and the shelves proved it.

The store was forty by sixty feet and the shelves that lined its walls were already half empty. Just ten days before, they had been stacked full with everything from clothes to shoes to toys to holiday decorations. Now the best stuff had been sold and what was left were the things that normally had to be deeply discounted to move. Yet people desperate for gifts were now buying those items at full price. This would be a Christmas to remember for the store's owner, Clark Miller, and one that Marge would never forget as well.

The two-inch-wide, round brass bell mounted atop the front door rang for the two hundredth time that day as Opal Stuart left Miller's with a shopping bag full of toys for her grandkids. As the sixty-year-old heavy leaded glass and oak door closed, Marge glanced around the building. For the first time all day, there were no customers to wait on. The only noise was the holiday music playing on the Aircastle radio located just behind her. Spinning in her two-inch heels, she turned the radio off. After taking a long, deep breath, she leaned against the counter and smiled. The building was suddenly as quiet as a church during a prayer meeting. The fact that there was no noise of footsteps, no squalling babies, no complaining old women or flirty young men, made this the best moment she'd had in days. Thank goodness, there were only two more shopping days until this mad rush was over.

As she relaxed for the first time since arriving at work, Marge noted someone else taking it easy too. Sitting off to one side of the store, on a round black stool behind the candy counter, was the store's owner. She knew Clark Miller had barely held onto the business during the Depression. Shortages during World War II had forced him to limp through those times as well. But now, happy days were here again. And though he'd just entered his fifth decade, this entire week he had paraded around with the zeal of a child who had been fed nothing but sugar for days. He was on top of the world!

Moving off the stool behind the counter, the big man ambled past a display of Christmas lights before arriving at Marge's station beside the main cash register. With a huge grin he all but shouted, "Guess I should have ordered more stuff."

She shook her head. "We wouldn't have had any place to put it. Besides, open the cash drawer. If we sell much more, there won't be room for the cash."

Miller smiled. "I like the way that sounds." Hitting a key, he grinned as the drawer popped out with a jingle. It had been a long time since he'd seen that much green. He fingered a few twenties before pushing it shut. Tapping the register's marble base, he posed a holiday question, "By the way, Marge, do you have electric lights for your Christmas tree? Boy, those eight-bulb, multicolored strands have been big sellers this year."

"No," she wearily replied, "we never had a set. We use some hand-me-down balls, a bit of tinsel, and popcorn strings to decorate our tree. Lights are a luxury we could never justify."

Miller folded his arms over his barrel chest and looked over at the few boxes of Noma lights left on the middle display island. With his dark three-piece suit, gold pocket watch chain dangling from the vest, white shirt, and red tie, he usually looked more like a banker than a shopkeeper. Yet at this moment, the whimsical expression on his chubby face cast him in the image of a very formal St. Nick. And his next statement cemented his standing as the town's Santa of the moment.

"Marge, grab a box of those lights and take them home with you. Christmas is about light, and you need to embrace that light. We all do! And maybe by putting those on your tree, it will brighten up the holidays for you and Jimmy."

"I'd love to have them," Marge softly replied, "but I couldn't afford to buy them. What little extra money I had went to a present for James—something he really needs. Maybe I can get some next year."

"Marge," Miller's tone was now scolding, "I'm not trying to sell you the lights. I'm giving them to you. Take home a box tonight. Your house, way out there in the country, must be a pretty dark place, at least at times. And with everybody coming home from the service except Robert, it might even be a bit darker this year."

Marge pushed herself upright and smiled. It was nice gesture, and maybe it would make things a bit better. But it was going to take a lot more than lights to brighten her world. She knew from his report cards and her talks with his teachers that James was in trouble. Though he didn't show out much at home, she sensed he was angry and she couldn't figure out why. Trying to understand his dramatic personality change had kept her awake at night. Now those painful thoughts were even invading her days.

"What's on your mind?" Miller asked.

"What?" Marge replied.

"You seem suddenly lost in thought."

"Oh," she answered, "it's probably nothing." She almost left it at that, but with the store empty and her heart troubled, she pushed her reddish hair off her forehead and spilled out her troubles in a series of short, quick bursts. "No, it is something. It's James. He seems to be angry and confused. His grades have fallen off. As much as I hate to admit it, he's not the kid he used to be. He doesn't hang out with his friends. He spends hours alone."

Miller let out a soft, short laugh, "Is that all? Marge, teenage boys go through this kind of stuff all the time. I know, I've had a couple of them. So don't beat yourself up. He'll shape up in a year or so and be back to the kid he was before the hormones kicked in. In fact, not only were Jed and Sam that way, so was I when I was Jimmy's age."

Marge glanced up at the sixteen-foot pressed tin ceiling. She'd been telling herself the same thing for the past two years, but she sensed her boy was different. It was more than just a bit of rebellion. This was something much deeper, and try as she could, he simply wouldn't talk to her about it.

The front door's bell pulled her from her trance. Glancing up she noted Audrey Lankins stroll over toward the sweater display. It was time to quit worrying about her boy and get back to work. If things with James didn't get better by summer, then she'd put together a plan. For the moment, it was far better to trust Clark Miller's advice. After all, he'd been through it a couple of times.

4

———— ❦ ————

December 21, 1945, 6:15 p.m.

James, did you cut that tree?"
It was funny how his mom was the one person in the world who would not call him Jimmy. She never had. Even while his dad had always called him Jimmy, his mother had refused. To her, he was always James.

Leaning back against the old, worn sofa, he shook his head, "Not yet, Mom. I don't even understand why we put one up. Just us two, and it seems a waste."

Her face drawn from her long day at work, Marge eased down into a wooden rocking chair beside the room's potbellied stove. She held her hands up to the warm cast iron for a moment, rubbing them together before sighing, "It just wouldn't be Christmas without a tree. Besides, I need to hang your father's star. That's an important part of our Christmas. We couldn't have Christmas without that. It reminds us who he was."

There was no dodging the fact she would again place that hunk of tin on the tree. A dozen of his classmates were actually spending Christmas with their dads while he'd be looking

———— ❦ ————

at that blasted award again, and yet so many thought he was the lucky one to have a father who gave his all for his country and won the Medal of Honor. If only they could walk in his shoes for a few days. If they could, they'd quickly understand that dying for your country, or anything else for that matter, was not a blessing. For those left behind, it was a curse—one that never left you alone and ate at you at least once a day and often more.

"I'll go out and find a tree tomorrow," Jimmy grudgingly assured her, as much to cut the talk of the medal as to get out of her doghouse.

"Thanks," Marge quietly said.

"What for?" Jimmy asked.

"The tree," she explained, a tired smile framing her face. "Tomorrow will be fine. It gives me time to make and string some popcorn and go through our ornaments. You want to help me? I'll let you eat as much as you string."

Pushing off the couch, Jimmy grabbed his coat and moved toward the front door. Without turning around he mumbled, "Not tonight, I'm going out, Mom."

"James," she said, her voice strong enough to cause him to turn in place, "where are you going?"

Uncomfortable under her gaze, he stood framed in the doorway and shrugged. "Some guys are going to go into town, just kind of hanging out and talking. We might play some pool. Nothing big. Johnny Barnett's coming by in a few minutes. He's got his uncle's truck. I told him I'd meet him at the end of the lane."

"You going to be late?" she quizzed.

"I won't be late, I promise."

She wearily pushed out of the chair and strolled over to the door. Smiling, she adjusted Jimmy's flannel shirt collar. "It's cold out there—the wind's pretty strong tonight. I heard on the radio today there was even a chance of snow. Be good to have a white Christmas."

"I guess," he replied.

"You know," she smiled, "I was gonna save this for Christmas Eve, but you need it now. No use saving it. You wait right here."

With no more explanation, she shuffled into her bedroom. As Jimmy rocked nervously by the door, he could hear her closet door opening. Thirty seconds later she was back, a large box wrapped in green and red tissue paper in her arms.

"You've needed this a long time," she sighed, pushing the box toward him.

He took it from her and stood at the door not moving.

"Open it, silly," she exclaimed, a childlike grin gracing a face that looked a decade older than it should have. Jimmy hated that she'd aged so much the past few years. She'd once been so young and pretty. No person should have to work as hard as she did. At times, he was too busy feeling sorry for himself to remember that. But at this moment he couldn't ignore that her life had also been tough since his dad's death. And here she was giving him something when she hadn't had a new dress or coat in years. It wasn't fair.

"Well?" she asked, twisting her apron in her hands. "You gonna open it or not?"

"Mom, you sound like a kid," he mumbled.

"I'm not too old to enjoy giving a gift," she shot back, her hazel eyes sparkling.

Moving over to the room's long end table, he set the gift on end and tore into the paper. Once a part of the box was exposed, he ripped the cardboard enough to reveal the contents. It was a green coat. How many extra hours had she worked to afford it?

"It's your school's colors," she proudly offered while stepping up to help him pull it out of the box. Tossing the now empty box to one side, she barked, "Now take off the old blue thing that you outgrew two years ago and slip this one on."

As he did, she proudly admired his every move. Once he had it on, she reached up and smoothed the shoulders. "You've grown up so much. You look so much like your father did when he was your age." Her fingers ran down the thin yellow stripes on the coat's collar.

"It's a nice coat, Mom," he assured her, pushing his hands into the garment's deep pockets. "I'll be really warm tonight."

"You stay out of trouble," she grinned as she reached up and kissed him on the cheek.

"You know me," he all but whispered as he turned to the door. He didn't look at her again for fear that she could read his thoughts; he didn't want her to know what he was really thinking. Just like he didn't want her to know what he was really doing tonight. Yet as he crossed from the yard to the gravel lane, he thought he could feel her eyes following his every move, and her lingering gaze, imagined or not, cut through his new coat and into his heart like a hot knife through butter. In a very real sense, that gaze was haunting him, the way Calvin's stories about his father did. Why couldn't folks just leave him alone? He didn't want to know how lucky he was or how great his dad had been. He just wanted all of them to leave him alone.

He was halfway down the lane when something stopped him in his tracks. Frozen in place, he glanced back to the house that held the memories he was trying to escape and then back to the road with its promise of a better life. He saw his mother's silhouette in the living room window. In spite of the trouble he'd been in at school, she had so much faith in him. Maybe he should be there to help her tonight. He was just about to head back to the house when he saw Johnny drive up and stop at the mailbox. As the north breeze cut through his cheeks, Jimmy grimly smiled. There was no turning back. He was about to join a very select club where few were invited and no one ever left.

Pulling his hands from the pockets of his new Kelly green coat, he sprinted down the lane toward his friend. There were people waiting for him, and he couldn't let them down.

5

December 21, 1945, 7:15 p.m.

As was still the case with many rural spots in this part of America, there was no electricity on the Anderson's property. When he'd been alive, Jacob Anderson hadn't wanted to pay for power. When he'd died four years before, no one had wanted to buy the old place either. The soil was so poor, all that would grow in the sandy clay was watermelon and peanuts, and it seemed the world had enough of both of those commodities.

After parking the truck behind a stand of trees, Johnny grinned, "This is it, man. We're about to hit the easy money."

Jimmy nodded but didn't answer. Even though World War II was over, a new, undeclared war was being fought for Johnny's soul, and the tug of war between the two combatants was literally yanking his heart in half. At the moment he wanted to turn around and walk away. Yet he couldn't do that. Like a coon in a wire trap, it was too late to rethink his options.

The boys silently got out and walked past the dilapidated house, only casually glancing toward the small cabin with its broken windows and half-open door. A few moments later, they ambled by a log barn, and then another hundred yards brought them to an old stable. Johnny and Jimmy stopped at a window and glanced in. The soft glow of a single hurricane oil lamp revealed a trio of ragged-looking men sitting on a rickety wooden bench. The unforgiving north wind literally blew through the clapboard siding, causing the trio to shiver and their oil lamp to flicker. Scattered around the men were a half dozen ancient rakes and hoes, a few wooden barrels that had once held molasses and about a dozen burlap grain sacks. Against the far wall was an antique wagon, its wooden sides weathered and its right front spoke wheel broken.

One of the men was large; his blocky face was littered with blemishes. He was dressed in an Army Air Corps leather jacket. He hardly looked the military type—he'd probably never seen the inside of the plane, so the coat was likely stolen or had come from a surplus store. The second man was small, squat, and clad in a checked coat like many lumbermen wore, yet he didn't look like he could pick up a six-foot axe, much less handle one. The final man, a skinny fellow with an angry scar on his left cheek, wore a Navy pea coat and dark blue slacks covered with grease stains. He could have easily played the small-time hood in a Bogart movie. Though the trio remained stone still and completely mute, their collective breath billowed in the cold winter air like steam coming from three locomotives.

The troubling scream of a rusty hinge caused each man to turn his eyes toward the building's only door. As it slowly swung open, the two visitors' forms filled the opening. No words were exchanged as the trio sized up their guests. Under the scrutiny, Jimmy and Johnny moved into the stable, letting the door slam behind them. Though new to the game, they seemed to understand the rules, and neither made any move to speak.

The shortest of the waiting men slowly yanked his lean body from the bench and moved closer to the lamp that rested on the wagon. His dark eyes flickered like a nervous neon sign as he studied the newcomers. Finally, after more than a minute where only the howls of the wind were heard, he spoke, his low, nasal voice carefully and threateningly emphasizing each of his words, "So you boys actually had the guts to show up."

Jimmy shoved his hands deep into his new coat's pockets and nodded. He was now sure this had not been a good idea. These out-of-towners were not his kind of people. They made the local moonshiners look classy. He couldn't help recalling a bit of his father's advice, "If you lie down with dogs, you get up with fleas." He figured he'd be scratching for a long time after tonight.

"I'm Jake," the man spat out, "and by showing up you're now in the corner. You can't walk out."

"Not planning to," Jimmy assured him. Though in truth he wanted to turn and sprint through the old door and down the long lane, his pride held him in place.

Jake casually ambled over to a spot just in front of the visitors, his eyes tracing the boys' forms as carefully as if measuring them for suits. After a few moments, he turned to the pair still holding down the bench. They both nodded. As they did, Jake whirled to again size up Jimmy.

"Here's the deal," the long, strained "e" in the final word highlighting a southern drawl far deeper than those native to Sharp county usually sported. "We only need you because your old lady works at the store. That makes it easier to do the job. Johnny told us she has a key to the building. Is that right?"

Jimmy nodded and glanced over at his friend. Johnny forced a smile before turning his gaze back toward Jake.

"And you can get it to us on Sunday afternoon?" Jake demanded. "Is that right?"

"Should be able to," Jimmy softly assured him.

Stepping up to where less than six inches separated them, the short man hissed, "'Should' doesn't cut it. Either you can or you can't. What is it?"

Holding his ground, Jimmy shot back, "I can get it."

"You'd better," the leader snarled. "That key makes this the easiest heist in history. Sunday night, while everyone's at the church program Johnny told us about, we walk into the store, pry open the old safe and help ourselves to the cash folks have been spending on holiday junk. Thanks to that key you're getting us, we don't have to make any noise or waste any time. We'll be out long before the program is over."

"What about the law?" Jimmy asked. "The sheriff's no dummy. In fact he's a pretty smart cookie."

Jake grinned, glancing back to his silent partners before continuing, "Johnny told us the sheriff's daughter is in the church program, so if he's any kind of good father, he'll be there. There'll be no law walking the streets that night until after the program. And Johnny will be at the program just to make sure he stays there. If he leaves, then Johnny will have a gun to take care of him before he gets to the store."

Jimmy glanced over at his friend. Johnny was smiling like a Cheshire cat. This had suddenly accelerated far beyond what he'd been told. Stealing a few dollars was one thing, but setting up to kill someone was a horse of a different color.

Yanking his hands from his pockets, Jimmy protested, "I'm not in this if it means hurting anyone. Don't mind taking some of Miller's cash, but I'm not going to be involved in killing Sheriff Thompson. He's a good guy and he's got three kids."

"So," Jake sneered, "then you better hope he's watching those kids at church. He'd better live by the motto, 'The family that prays together stays together.'"

While the trio and Johnny laughed, Jimmy remained stone silent. It was then he noticed the pistol stuffed in Jake's belt. The little man also noticed that his weapon had been spotted.

"Like it?" Jake grinned, pulling it out and pointing it toward Jimmy. "You don't follow through and I'll use it on you. You're a part of this now. If anything goes wrong, the sheriff won't be the only one laying on the cold frozen ground. You got it, country boy?"

"Yeah," Jimmy assured him, "I understand."

He also understood he was in over his head. It was just like when he was seven. He and some boys had been playing in the river down by the blue hole. Jimmy climbed a fifty-foot cliff and launched himself toward the water. It was only after he was in the air that he realized he hadn't fully thought out his jump. What if the water was too shallow? As it turned out, the depth was fine, but the undertow was much stronger than any of the boys imagined. He was literally in over his head and was not strong enough to break the river's hold on him. Fortunately his father had picked that moment to hike over to the river and check things out. Without his dad diving in and pulling him out of the river, Jimmy would have likely drowned.

Tonight he'd again leapt in without thinking and the danger was likely just as deadly. But this time his father wasn't there to pull him out.

As Jimmy tried to figure out an escape clause in this unholy contract, the taller of the trio pushed his body from the bench and grabbed a jug from the wagon's bed. He pulled a cork from the dark bottle with his teeth, spit it onto the floor, took a long draw, and sighed. His grin revealed a gap where his front two teeth should have been. With no warning, he tossed the bottle to Jake, who caught it in his left hand. After taking a quick sip, the short man gave it to Johnny. The teen wasted no time downing a swallow and pushed the bottle toward Jimmy.

"No, thanks," Jimmy said.

"Too good to drink with us?" Jake barked.

"No," Jimmy barked back, "too smart. If I got caught with moonshine on my breath, my mom would watch me like a hawk. If I'm going to get her key, I have to play this thing right."

The short man grabbed the bottle from Johnny, took another long swig and, after the booze had cleared his throat, smiled, and said, "Smart move, kid. You should be just fine on this job. I like a man who thinks before he acts. Now come over here by the lamp and I'll outline the plan."

Jimmy and Johnny followed Jake back to the wagon. Ten minutes later, after the man had given them a blow-by-blow description of what to expect in their first foray into the world of real crime, the meeting was dismissed.

The boys had passed the barn and the house before Johnny finally found his voice. "Going to be an easy way to pick up fifty bucks and maybe a lot more."

"As long as we don't get caught," Jimmy replied, opening the truck's door and sliding into the passenger seat. Those words reflected the boy's biggest fear. It was easy to rationalize taking old man Miller's money. After all, the guy worked his mother hard and paid her very little. But what if something went wrong? It would kill his mother, and Jimmy hadn't slid far enough to want to hurt her. Not yet, anyway!

And then there was the matter of Sheriff Thompson. He was one of the nicest people in the world. His daughter Suzy was in Jimmy's class at school. If anything happened to him, Jimmy would never be able to live with himself.

"Kind of funny when you think about it," Johnny chuckled.

"What's funny?" Jimmy shot back.

"That we planned a Christmas heist in a stable."

To Jimmy, it was anything but funny. In fact, the thought suddenly chilled him even more deeply than the north wind.

6

———⊸∞⊷———

December 21, 1945, 7:45 p.m.

I can't believe this," Johnny moaned as he studied the truck's flat front tire. "I'm going to get in so much trouble!"

Jimmy shook his head; trouble was the name of the game they were playing. If a flat tire on a truck was cause for alarm, just think of the price getting caught robbing a store or shooting a sheriff would bring. So why was his friend so panicked over a little thing like this? It was just a hunk of rubber attached to a six-year-old truck.

"Calm down, Johnny," Jimmy barked. "All we have to do is put the spare on and get going. No big deal."

"No," the other boy cried, "it's so much bigger than that! This is the spare. I already had one flat today."

"So?" Jimmy laid a hand firmly on his friend's shoulder as he spoke, "Your uncle will understand. He knows what these roads do to tires."

The now completely rattled kid shook his head. "He doesn't know I have the truck."

It was suddenly all too apparent; Johnny's first venture into larceny had started well before the Miller's Store job. The

———⊸∞⊷———
42

kid must have just taken the truck hoping that no one would notice. It was not the stupidest stunt Jimmy had ever known Johnny to pull, but it was in the top five.

"But you told me . . ."

Johnny cut Jimmy's remarks short by kicking the tire and spitting out a long stream of curse words.

"Yeah, that fixes everything," Jimmy grumbled. Glancing down U.S. 62 toward Agnos, he shook his head. What a day this was turning out to be! His partner in crime was crying like a baby, the clouds were spitting snow, and it was going to be a long, cold four-mile walk home. Turning his new coat's collar up over his neck, Jimmy glanced back at his friend. "Let's start moving. I got no hankering to freeze on the side of the road."

"You can," Johnny stubbornly shot back, "but I'm staying here with the truck. I can't leave it out along the side of the road. Some thief might grab it! There are all kinds of people just looking for a person to drop their guard. When they do, they steal you blind!"

Turning his back to the wind, it was all Jimmy could do not to break out in a smile. His friend's words really hit home. After all, Johnny had already started down that same path as those who'd steal the old Dodge. After taking a deep breath, Jimmy sighed, "Come on, Johnny. Just grab the keys and it'll be fine."

"You don't know my uncle. He'd just knock me around a little for using his truck, but he'd pulverize me if I deserted it. I'll sit in the cab. In a couple of hours, when he and his buddies get finished playing poker in town, they'll come by here and stop."

Jimmy watched Johnny march resolutely back to the side of the truck, slide behind the wheel, and slam the door. Waving a hand more in disgust than in farewell, he turned his face into the wind and began the hike home. As he stared into the darkness, he couldn't help but wonder if the band of confederates he'd joined up with were bright enough to pull this off. Ten minutes later that question was haunting him so deeply it froze him in his tracks. Turning, he looked back toward the place where Johnny was waiting in the old truck. As he tried to peer through the snow and darkness, Mr. Wiles's warning howled at him through the wind. The words had an even greater impact now than they did on the school steps.

"I've seen it before. Starts with stuff like breaking windows, sneaking behind the fence to smoke, and getting drunk, but it always ends with a whole lot more. And you're heading that way at a breakneck pace."

7

December 21, 1945, 8:15 p.m.

*H*e'd made about a half mile, his body chilled by the wind and snow, when he heard the sound of a vehicle behind him. Moving to the side, Jimmy glanced back over his shoulder and saw two dim lights topping a hill and moving toward him. This might be Johnny's uncle and his gang, and if that were the case, it would probably be better to hide than meet up with them. Yet the thought of facing another three and a half miles of road on foot was far more discouraging than dealing with the former Army private's wrath. So, stepping slightly to the side, the boy waved his arms to catch the driver's attention, only halting his wild motions when the old sedan slowed and rolled to a stop at the spot where Jimmy stood on the shoulder.

As the car idled, the driver's window came down and a familiar voice called out, "You need a lift?"

Jimmy had never been so happy to hear Calvin's happy twang. Without saying a word, the boy hustled across the road, yanked the door open, and slid into the passenger seat.

The bus driver's '34 Ford might be old and worn, but at this moment it was as inviting as a new Caddy.

"Saw Johnny back a ways. He told me you were walking home. You must've been moving pretty fast, I expected to run across you sooner than I did."

"The wind was a great motivator," Jimmy explained as he closed the door. "Boy, I appreciate this."

"Glad to have you aboard," came the cheerful reply as the man let out on the clutch and eased back onto the highway, "but I can't take you straight home. I'm on a mission tonight, and I can't complete that mission until I pick a few things up at my house. So I hope you don't mind killing a bit of time with me."

"Beats walking," Jimmy laughed.

"Glad to have the company," the driver said with a smile.

The Ford turned off Highway 62 and rumbled down what seemed to be little more than a footpath. Tree limbs rubbed against the car's fabric top, and deep ruts caused the suspension to shake and moan like the Ghost of Christmas Past. Three minutes and four cattle guards from the main road, Calvin finally eased the sedan past a chicken coop and up to a tiny white frame house.

"This is home," he happily announced as he shut off the motor. "Get on out and follow me inside. We won't be long. My place is kind of drafty, but it'll be warmer in there than out in this old jalopy."

Since it was off the beaten path, Jimmy had never been to Calvin's house. As he climbed out of the car and sized up the place, it was about what could be expected for a man who was just trying to hold onto a poor piece of land. The weather-beaten house was tiny, probably not more than five hundred square feet. It didn't even have a porch, just four rickety steps that led up to a two-by-four-foot stoop. There was no lock on the front door and a quick look into the house showed why. There was simply nothing worth stealing. The furniture was old and worn, probably not as much secondhand as fifth- or sixth-hand. The small living room's only padded furniture was a short couch sporting a faded, torn quilt tossed over the seats. It was likely there to cover holes in the original green fabric similar to those on the piece's top cushions. The clapboard structure was heated by an iron potbellied stove set between the front room and the tiny kitchen. Not far behind that stove was a single bare light hanging down from the ceiling over the center of the crude piece of sanded, square pine that served as the owner's table. The Depression might have officially ended five or six years before, but that news hadn't gotten to this location.

Though it was warmer in the house than it was outside, Jimmy still felt a deep chill as he stepped into the front room. There was no reason to unbutton his coat. Calvin pushed by him, grabbed a couple of pieces of wood from beside the stove, opened the stove's door with his gloved hand, and tossed in the hickory logs. After pushing a few coals around with a poker, he closed the door, pulled off his gloves, and moved back to the table. Pushing one of the two ladder-back chairs away from the table, he eased down, momentarily studying what sat on the table in front of him—a small wooden object.

Moving past the stove and into the room, Jimmy observed Calvin gently running a finger over a six-inch piece of walnut. The man smiled and nodded, his brown eyes sparkling as he studied his work under the dim light. Without looking up, he set the object of his affection back on the table and spoke, "Just think, more than a hundred years ago a seed sprouted on a hill about a half mile from this house. It grew for a century, reaching sixty feet from the ground toward the sky. It survived hot dry summers, long cold winters, thunderstorms, ice storms, and tornadoes."

The older man, wrinkles now as deep as the ruts in a muddy dirt road, glanced toward his guest with a look of childlike wonder etched on his weathered face, "Think of all the walnuts it produced. Those nuts fed countless generations of animals while making our human diets a bit better too. Then a few years back, during an incredible thunderstorm, lightning struck this old relic." Calvin smiled and snapped his fingers. "Just like that it quit producing food or shade or much of anything else. It died and yet in a very real sense that tree's magic continues."

Glancing toward Jimmy, he picked up the small piece of wood and handed it to the boy. "Look at it, son. It took a hundred years to make that."

Jimmy studied the object he'd been given. It was no longer just a piece of a tree; it had been transformed into something far different. The bus driver had shaped this small chunk of ancient wood into a candleholder. After carving it, it had been carefully sanded and stained. Then he must have spent hours polishing it because it caught and reflected every bit of the room's muted light. A place in the top had been bored out to hold a candle. The base was flat to set it on a table.

As he rolled the piece of craftsmanship in his hands, Jimmy suddenly noted something that had initially been hidden in his palm. On one side of the candleholder Calvin had carved a star into the wood. But there was more! Raising the piece until it was just a few inches from the light, he noted that in the middle of that star was a word—HOPE!

"You did this?" Jimmy asked as he handed the carving back to his host.

Calvin nodded and smiled modestly before placing it with at least a dozen others in a cardboard box. With no further words of explanation, the bus driver gently picked up the box, tucked it under his right arm, pushed his chair back from the table, and stood. A few seconds later, Jimmy followed the man out the door and into the car. It was only after Calvin had set the box between them; started the Ford; rattled down the long, almost invisible lane; and pulled back out on the highway the boy asked the obvious question.

"Why did you make so many?"

The older man shrugged, his eyes, now illuminated by the car's very basic instrumentation, never leaving the road, "They're for some folks who live alone. They're also for those who don't have family around here and therefore have no one to share Christmas with them. So in that way their holidays are filled with darkness. This is my way of bringing a bit of hope and light into their world."

Jimmy let the man's words sink in. In the past few hours, he'd discovered there was a lot more to Calvin than he or the other kids who rode his bus could have guessed. As his grandfather would have said, this man had layers and it was time to find out what those layers contained.

"Can I ask another question?"

"Sure!" Calvin readily replied.

"How long did it take you to make them? I mean, you must have been working on these for weeks."

"Actually," the man's tone revealed a humble amusement, "I work on them all year. It gives me something to do as I listen to the radio at night. So I don't count the hours."

As the car chugged along the dirt path back to the highway, Jimmy glanced back at Calvin, "Do you get much money for them?"

Calvin grinned, shook his head, and patted the car's banjo-style steering wheel. "I hadn't thought of that," he chuckled.

"No, I don't make them to sell, I make them for folks on my Christmas list."

The boy shook his head. Calvin didn't have any family. There was no one he really hung around with. So why make so many?

"I can see what you're thinking," the driver said as he turned back onto the highway. "After all, I've got no wife and kids. My folks are dead, and the only brother I have lives in California. So you're wondering who in the world is on my list."

"Yeah," Jimmy admitted.

"Jimmy," Calvin began, "the folks I make them for are all around us. In fact, you ride past them when I drive your school bus route. But like most of the world, you just don't see them. You look down the highway, your eyes fixed on getting home. That's nothing to be ashamed of, that's just the way most folks are. That's the nature of busy people in a busy world. They are so busy seeing what is in front of them they fail to see what's all around them."

"Never thought about it," Jimmy replied.

"Let me put it another way," Calvin offered. "There are people you know who can't walk past a mirror without staring at what is reflected there. Now let me ask you this, what do you see when you look in a mirror?"

The boy paused for a moment, wondering if this was a trick question. As he pondered the man's query, he could see the one obvious answer, "I see me."

"Actually," Calvin chuckled, "you really don't see yourself. You see a reverse image of yourself. But that's not the point. The point is we live in a world where most of us spend a lot more time looking in the mirror, by that I mean seeing our own desires and needs, than we do looking out the window at the world. You have to look out the window to see where you're needed. A mirror just can't show you that."

The driver let his words settle in for a moment, then raised his right hand and tapped the car's rearview mirror.

"Jimmy, what do you think I see when I look into that glass?"

"What's behind us!"

"Yep, that's what a mirror does. It shows us where we've been. I'm a lot more interested in seeing where I'm going. So when I drive on the out-of-the-way back roads in my old school bus, I'm not focusing on just one spot, I'm keeping my eyes open and trying to see the whole picture. And by looking around, it's pretty easy for me to see folks who need something."

Jimmy recalled one of the weird things about the bus route. Almost every day, including today, one of the front seats was filled with a cardboard box or two that didn't belong to the kids. Tilting his head to the side, the boy connected the dots and said, "The eggs, the cured hams, the other stuff you always have on the bus in those boxes, that's why you stop at places where kids don't live. You are giving that stuff away."

"Sharing it," Calvin corrected him. His eyes shining, he posed a final question, "You mind going in with me as I deliver a couple of these trinkets? I need to turn off the road and go down toward the Shorts' place. I guarantee it's not far and it won't take long."

"You're the driver," Jimmy quipped. "I'm just lucky not to be walking home."

"By the way," Calvin asked, "did you read that verse I told you about?"

"No," the kid admitted. Then as an afterthought he added, "I didn't have the time."

"Well," the grinning driver explained, "this is what it says—there is no greater thing to do than to lay down your life for someone else. It means more than just dying for someone, it also means living for others as well."

Jimmy nodded.

"Yep," Calvin said, "when you live for others, you start to realize all the blessings you have. It might be hard for you to believe after seeing my house, but I'm kind of rich in some ways."

8

December 21, 1945, 9:10 p.m.

The road, one that Jimmy had been down countless times on the school bus, seemed much bumpier at night. As it navigated the ruts cut deeply into the red clay, the old Ford rocked so violently from side to side its passengers felt like juggler's props. Somehow, Calvin's hands stayed on the steering wheel, and miraculously the four tires always came back down on the road without exploding. About a half mile off the main highway, Calvin headed the V-nosed car down an almost hidden lane Jimmy had never noticed before. The narrow path wound back through the woods a quarter mile before ending in front of a cabin whose only alterations from pioneer times seemed to be the concrete added for chinking between the hand-hewn logs. Switching off the motor and lights, the driver blew the horn twice, grabbed one of the candleholders, and, with no warning or explanation, pushed the driver's door open. Jimmy followed suit on the passenger side and trailed behind Calvin as he crossed a rocky yard now sporting about a half-inch of fresh snow. The older man momentarily stopped his purposeful trek when he stepped up onto a plank porch.

He stomped a couple of times to knock the snow from his shoes and then turned slowly toward the front door. As he did, it opened, and waiting at the entry was a white-haired woman holding a kerosene lantern. Wrapped in a handmade shawl and wearing a dress likely made out of old flour sacks, she was bent and wrinkled, but the dim light showed a full set of white teeth and those teeth reflected a smile that came close to being a substitute for a porch lamp.

"Calvin," her tone was a mix of a mother's scolding and a neighbor's welcome, "you shouldn't have come out on a night like this one."

"I had to," he replied. "Got something for you, Miss Masie."

Slowly turning and moving back into her one-room home, she motioned for her guests to join her. After stepping just inside the ancient plank door, Calvin handed the candle-holder to the old woman. Then, as if a magical spell had been cast, time seemed to stop. As the bus driver's eyes hung on each barely perceptible move, the woman's thin fingers traced the man's work, her head nodding approval as tears welled up in the corners of her eyes. Only after silently mouthing the word carved into the wood did she choke out, "You never forget me."

"Miss Masie," Calvin's reply was likely an explanation she'd heard a hundred times before but it still sounded fresh, sincere, and unrehearsed, "I wouldn't have ever made it through eighth grade if you hadn't stayed after school each day to work with me on math." A childlike grin covering his jaw, he reached into his coat and retrieved an envelope. "Here's a card for you too."

After wiping her eyes with her sleeve, the old woman took the envelope and, rather than open it, tucked it into her belt.

In an apologetic tone she sighed, "I don't have anything for you."

"I still owe you for all you've done for me," the man assured her. "I can never fully pay you back, Miss Masie."

The woman's expression clearly showed she wasn't buying Calvin's explanation, and her eyes also conveyed that this gift was just another of many he had presented to her over who knows how many years. Shaking her head, she set the candleholder on the room's only table and glanced toward the companion who had come with her former student.

"Who is this young fellow?" she asked.

"Jimmy Reed," came the quick explanation. "You remember his dad, the guy who won the Medal of Honor. Jimmy's kind of like that candleholder I carved for you, he was cut from a good piece of wood."

"Guess that means he's pretty solid too," the woman added with a wink.

Those words that brought a smile to Calvin and Miss Masie cut Jimmy to the bone. Though the fireplace hadn't done much to heat up the tiny cabin, the boy suddenly felt a line of sweat beading on his brow. If they knew what he was a part of, they wouldn't be smiling. If they knew what was going to happen on Sunday night, they also likely wouldn't trust being with him. Thankfully, Calvin's next announcement offered the reprieve and relief Jimmy needed to escape the tiny cabin and the claustrophobic cloud that was now creeping into his head and squeezing his conscience.

"Now, Miss Masie, we have to get going. I've got one more stop to make, and then I need to get Jimmy home before it's too late. I don't want his mother worrying about him."

"God bless you, Calvin," she softly said, "and nice meeting you, Mr. Reed."

Moving toward the door, Calvin smiled and offered a hearty, "Merry Christmas." And suddenly the man and boy were again out in the cold, back in the car, and headed to the next mysterious destination. Except for the almost silent flathead V-8 engine and the whisper of the wind through the trees, the night was as quiet as a tomb.

The next mile down the road took more than five minutes to traverse. Heavy fall rains had washed off much of the gravel while logging trucks had created a mishmash of deep channels in the red clay and rocks that remained. The Ford fought through them with the determination of a salmon swimming upstream to spawn, yet Jimmy couldn't help but wonder how the sedan kept from breaking an axle as it bounced from rut to rut. The ride only got worse as Calvin turned left onto an unmarked lane that likely had known few motorized vehicles. A hundred yards later the car rolled to a stop beside a tiny native stone house. This time Calvin didn't sound his horn to alert the home's occupants he had arrived. As his hand grabbed the door handle, he shot a stern look at his rider. There was just enough light to prove the man had something very serious on his mind.

"Big Joe and Marie Foster live here. You've probably never seen them in town. Because of the color of their skin, we really don't let them into the stores or the like, at least not the front of the stores anyway. What few friends and family they have left back in the twenties. Some went to Memphis, others New Orleans and a few Chicago. But they stayed here, eking out a living off the land and eating whatever they could grow in their fields, hunt with their rifle, or catch with a cane pole. But if you aren't going to treat them with the same respect you do white folks, then you just stay in the car. You understand?"

"I've never been in a Negro's house," Jimmy almost whispered, a hint of fear in his voice.

"It's just like yours and mine, and the folks who live in this home are a lot better than most of the people you've ever met. It's up to you—are you going or staying?"

"Going," came the nervous reply.

Once again, Jimmy followed his guide up onto the porch. After only one knock, the door opened. Filling the entryway was a huge black man dressed in bib overalls. He must have been six and a half feet tall and at least two hundred and fifty pounds. His voice was deep enough to start an earthquake.

"Mr. Cal, what brings you out on a night like this, as if I didn't know. Get in this house and out of that wind."

"Thanks, Joe, hope you don't mind that I brought a friend with me tonight. You knew his dad. This is Robert Reed's boy, Jimmy."

The big man's face broke out into a toothy smile. "Lordy, your dad was about the finest human being I ever knew. What a pleasure it is to lay my poor old eyes on his offspring."

As Jimmy approached, Joe stuck out a right hand that was as big as a country-cured ham. Jimmy's own hand was promptly swallowed up when they shook. The vigorous shaking that followed didn't stop until all three men were standing inside the home's small living room. Beside the fire, sitting in a wooden rocker, was the other member of the family. Dressed in a starched and pressed yellow dress, her hair pulled back in a neat bun, Marie was as small as Joe was large. She couldn't have measured more than four-and-a-half-feet tall and probably didn't weigh ninety pounds. Her skin was Hershey chocolate brown, her eyes as black as the night, and her face showed few signs of the hard life Jimmy was sure she must have endured. Only after they entered and the front door had been shut, did she stand and face them.

"Brother Cal," she began, her voice robust but sweet, "it's been too long since we've had you in our home."

Striding earnestly past Jimmy, the bus-driving farmer was quickly enveloped in the tiny woman's arms. This hug was long, the type usually reserved more for members of the family than for casual acquaintances.

"Merry Christmas, Marie," Calvin finally said as he patted the woman's tiny back.

"Lord bless you," she whispered. As the hug ended, she added, "And a big welcome to you, Brother Jimmy. Would you all like a cup of cocoa or maybe a piece of butter cake? I made some real fine fudge today too."

A huge smile punctuated Calvin's quick response, "My goodness, Marie, sad to say I got to get this boy home. So we don't have to time to stay and eat, but if you wanted to send a bit of fudge home with me, I'd surely love that."

The woman nodded and moved with the grace of a cat toward the kitchen counter to her right. As she did, Calvin turned to face Joe.

"It's not really much," he apologized, "but I wanted you to have this candleholder. I know you always light a candle at midnight each Christmas Eve."

Eyes beaming, Joe gently took the gift in his big right mitt. "Look, Mama, what he done made for us. Isn't it fine?"

After finishing wrapping the peanut butter fudge in an old cloth, Marie set the candy on the counter and touched her husband's arm. A few seconds later, her hand found the candleholder. She traced it with the index finger of her left hand, smiled, and announced, "A star."

"That's right," Calvin confirmed.

She continued to trace her way across the wooden base until she noticed something else about the star. Tilting her head to the left, she nodded and whispered, "Hope."

"Miss Marie, you can see as good with your hands as I can see with my eyes."

She giggled, brought her fingers together and exclaimed, "Does that mean this old blind woman could drive a bus as good as you?"

Joe howled, "That's something I'd like to see."

Jimmy hadn't noticed the woman was blind. She'd looked at him when she spoke, and she'd moved across to the kitchen with the grace of a dancer. She had him fooled so deeply he still wondered if he was being led on.

"I have to get the boy home," Calvin almost apologetically explained.

"I understand," Joe said, "but would you at least come back and share Christmas dinner? We'd be honored to have you eat turkey with us. That is, if I can find one to shoot between now and then."

"Christmas night?" Calvin asked.

"About six," Joe offered.

"I'll be here," he assured them. "Now, Marie, where's my fudge?"

After grabbing the fudge off the counter and sharing another hug, Calvin led the way back to the car. Joe stood on the porch, waving that big hand until the Ford made its way back to the road. Only then did the large man step back into the small home and close the door.

As they headed back to the Reed farm, Jimmy was lost in thought, and his thoughts stoked questions that both confused and troubled him. Thus, when the sedan pulled to a stop at the end of the lane, he didn't immediately jump from the car. Instead he licked his lips and haltingly asked, "Why?"

Calvin turned toward him and smiled. "You don't go to church much . . . do you?"

Jimmy shook his head, "Not since Dad died. Mom works six days a week, and Sunday she has so much to do—you know, stuff she doesn't get to do during the week."

"I understand," he told the boy. "There's no need to apologize. But there is a passage in Matthew that seems to give me purpose and hope. You got a Bible?"

"Sure," Jimmy answered, "we used to read out of it at Christmas until Dad died."

Calvin smiled and continued, "Why I do what I do is all about the least of these . . . you know, those folks who have a lot less than we do. It's like when I touch them I've been given the privilege and honor of holding that baby who was born so long ago in a manger. I think it's kind of like wrapping God in your arms. Can you understand why that means so much to me?"

Jimmy didn't have a clue, and his face displayed that ignorance. This was almost like a foreign language, and he simply couldn't come to grips with motivation this simple and direct.

"Don't worry about it now," Calvin smiled as he spoke. "When it's time, you'll figure it out. Anyway, I made one of these candleholders for you and your mom. Maybe it can kind of be your guide to finding what I just talked about. If you'll pardon the pun, maybe it can light your way." He punctuated his explanation with a quick chuckle and reached into the box to pull out one of the carved pieces of walnut. Handing it to the boy, he smiled and said, "Good night, Jimmy."

The boy nodded, pushed the Ford's door open, and stepped out onto solid ground to begin his short trek to the porch. As he reached the steps, he turned to watch Calvin drive down the long lane to the highway. It was only when the Ford's small red taillights faded into the darkness that he noticed the snow had stopped and the skies had suddenly cleared. A thousand bright stars greeted him as he gazed toward the heavens. Something had happened; he didn't understand it, but there was something different. It was a feeling, and for the moment, he couldn't define what it meant.

9

December 22, 1945, 8:07 a.m.

He had been glad his mother was asleep when he got in. The fact she had to get up early to catch her ride to town for work meant he didn't have to answer a long list of questions as to how his night had been. Yet while his mother wasn't the one asking, the troubling questions were still tossing very hard jabs that had kept him awake until the part of the day farmers called the milking hour. It was then sleep finally came, but now, as he rolled out of bed just after eight, he felt exhausted. Jimmy found three cold biscuits and a couple of pieces of ham on the table. Pulling a jar of dark molasses from the cupboard, he ate in silence. Maybe it was because of the troubled state of his mind that the food seemed tasteless.

Though he had all day—and since the animals had been sold off, his chores were light—he immediately dug into his Saturday routine. After moving a wheelbarrow full of firewood from beside the shed to the front porch, and then stacking the firewood beside the door, he grabbed a bow saw and his gloves and headed off to a tree-covered field on the back forty. Several weeks before, when he'd hunted squirrels, he'd come across a five-foot high tree that was just thin enough to fit in their living room beside the stove and just full enough to hold all their ornaments.

The ten-minute walk past the pond, along an old wagon trail, through a small stand of free-growing cane, and to the banks of Hickory Creek was usually one he enjoyed, but today was anything but a normal day. Even spotting a few wild turkeys did nothing to lift him from his foul mood. He was trapped in a jail he had constructed, voluntarily entered, and then locked. One impulsive move was all it had taken. Without thinking of the real consequences, he had joined a gang, and he was the reason they could pull off a near-perfect job. All it took was a key he could easily lift from his mother's purse. When Johnny had first told him about it, it seemed so perfect. But now reality had set in. What if something went wrong? What if he didn't get the key back into his mom's purse and she found out he had taken it? What then?

The thought of disappointing her was even worse than the reality of jail time if he was caught. Her heart had already been broken once when his father had been killed, but eventually that had been tempered by the fact he'd been recognized as a hero. This time, if her heart were broken, the reality would be that Jimmy was a criminal. There would be no escaping that. People would whisper, point fingers, talk about how she had failed the boy. They would likely blame her even more than him. He couldn't live with that.

Trying to shake the image of her tears and humiliation from his mind, Jimmy turned his attention to what he could do with the money if everything did come off as promised. The first thing would be to get his mother a real present—perhaps a new dress or shoes or maybe even both. He could get Audrey something too. There was some perfume she always talked about. He could just see her face when he presented it to her.

Yeah, those thoughts made the risk almost seem worth taking. Almost. But all the presents he could buy couldn't completely shake the hounds of fear that were hot on his trail. Their yapping was so loud he already felt like a wanted man.

Perhaps it was his foreboding sense of shame that pushed the present out of his thoughts or maybe just his coat's upturned collar that obscured his view, but he almost marched by the little one that cried out to be this year's special tree. It was only tripping over a rock and falling against an oak that woke him up to the moment and his surroundings. And there, just a stone's throw to his right, was the object of his quest.

Moving toward the evergreen, he reevaluated his choice. One side was a bit uneven—he could trim and shape that with some clippers—but the height and girth were about right. Walking around it proved there were no dead spots either. This one would do just fine. He had dropped to his knees to find the best place to cut when a voice called out from the other side of the creek.

"Jimmy Reed. What you doing out in the woods this time of the morning? Looking for rabbits?"

Turning his eyes toward the spot where the voice originated, Jimmy noted a classmate, Amos Ward, standing beside a post oak tree, a .22 rifle casually resting over his right shoulder. Amos was kind of a misfit. He'd flunked a couple of grades and was now just being carried along by the teachers' goodwill. Without extra credit for cleaning the chalkboards and bringing in wood for the gym's stoves, he'd never pass anything. Nevertheless, in spite of the fact he wasn't really all there, the short, stout kid with the big smile was a peach. He was honest, happy, and direct. As Wylie Rhoads always said, "Amos was a character, but he also had character."

Bringing himself to his feet, Jimmy gave a half-hearted salute and yelled back, "Just cutting a Christmas tree for Mom. What are you up to?"

"Looking for supper. Mom told me to bring home something she could cook."

"I saw some turkey back toward our pond," Jimmy suggested.

"That'd be great," Amos, his answer framed by a huge grin, replied. "If I could get two, we could have something for Christmas dinner too. Thanks."

The boy turned to his left and took two steps before stopping and glancing back at Jimmy. Waving his hand, he yelled out, "Guess you heard about Johnny Barnett?"

The mere mention of the name caused a cold chill to race down Jimmy's spine. Whatever the news, he figured it was something he wasn't going to want to hear. Yet he had to know.

"What about Johnny?" Jimmy hollered back. "Something happen to him?"

Amos nodded, "He didn't get hurt or nothing, but he sure did get into some powerful trouble. He stole his uncle's truck and ruined two tires. I understand his dad took a strap to him and his mom pretty much confined him to his room until school starts after New Year's. About the only place he can go is the kitchen table and the outhouse until then."

There was no reason to ask another question. Jimmy had all the information he needed. Johnny's career in crime had begun and ended yesterday. He was no longer a part of the team. And as it was Johnny who'd brought Jimmy into the game, Jimmy would be operating with no one he knew or in any way trusted. As he watched Amos trudge up the far side of the creek bank, he took stock of his situation. It was obvious he needed to find a way out of this mess, but was that even possible? Last night Jake had carefully and forcefully explained there was no walking away. Once he entered that stable, he was trapped. Nothing short of a miracle could save him now.

Falling back to his knees, he took his frustrations out on the tree. Perhaps due to his anxiety-fueled energy more than the saw's sharp edge, the tree came down in just under two minutes. As he grabbed the now fallen tree by the trunk and dragged it along the trail back home, he began to wonder if he was about to be cut down to size just as quickly.

10

December 22, 1945, 1:10 p.m.

Ash Flat was about six miles up the road from the Reeds' farmhouse. Even though the town was in the Ozark foothills, the road between Agnos and the county seat was cut along fairly level ground. Even though the sun was shining, the wind calm, and the temperatures in the low forties, it still would have been a very long, two-hour walk for even a young, tough kid like Jimmy. Normally, due to the fact that he lived in a place that was well off the beaten path, there were usually few folks driving down the gravel road. Yet this was not just another Saturday, this was the Saturday before Christmas, so the normally placid Highway 62 was alive with traffic heading to town to visit and shop. He had no more than walked down the family's long lane and across to the far side of the road when a 1937 Dodge truck topped the hill behind him, downshifted into second, and slowed to a stop where the boy was standing.

"Need a ride to town?" Asked a tall, thin man dressed in a pair of union-made Hercules bib overalls and a white dress shirt.

Jimmy sized the dark-headed stranger up as a farmer, not just from his dress, but also the full milk cans lining the back of the truck. Jimmy knew he must be on his way to town to deliver this morning's take. "I'd appreciate a lift," he replied, the still-nagging guilt over the pending robbery forcing him into an insincere smile.

"My name's Collins," the man announced as he reached across the cab to push the passenger door open.

"I'm Jimmy Reed," the boy answered as he stepped up on the running board and slid onto the cab's bench seat. Like most teenage boys, he loved cars and trucks, so his eyes were initially drawn to the vehicle's centrally located instrument panel. Four small rectangular gauges were set in the middle of the metal dash and were framed by two round gauges on either side. Just below the instrument cluster was the floor-mounted shifter topped by a large black knob. The truck must have been repainted at some point, the shine was too deep to be factory issue and Jimmy had never seen a Dodge sporting green paint with red pinstripes. For a farm tool, it was pretty special!

"Glad to have you aboard, Jimmy," Collins said. "Anywhere in particular you need to be dropped in town?"

"Yeah, my mom works at Miller's Store. Somewhere close to there would be great!"

"I'm going right by that place," the older man assured the boy as the old truck picked up speed. "I'll drop you right at the front door."

As Collins eased the truck down the highway, it quickly became obvious that he was immersed in the holiday spirit. Softly at first, the farmer began humming the old holiday standard "Jingle Bells," and when he got to the chorus, he actually began to sing the lyrics. The mood was infectious, as within a mile Jimmy was mouthing the words too. It appeared the number was just about to build into a robust duet when, with no warning, the man slammed on the brakes, almost throwing Jimmy into the cab's windshield and causing milk cans to bang across the back of the cab. As the vehicle skidded to a stop, Collins shoved the transmission into neutral, set the emergency brake, flung open the driver's door, and jogged over to the edge of the woods. He stopped at a small hackberry tree and studied one of the branches as if he were a tree doctor. Reaching into his pocket, he retrieved a pocketknife and cut off a small green growth from one of the tree's bottom limbs. After shoving the knife back into his overalls, he walked back to the truck and reentered the cab.

"Sorry about charging off like that," he said as he laid the six-inch green plant on the seat between them, "but I've been looking for a good specimen all week. It's just not Christmas without it."

As the man eased the truck back down the road, Jimmy took a gander at the strange plant that had seemingly brought such great joy to Collins. Over the years he'd seen plenty of these berry-laden parasites, but he'd never really paid much attention to them and certainly had never had any desire to stop a trip just to retrieve a sample. So why in the world would this man think this piece of greenery was so important? Collins's happy drumming on the steering wheel shifted Jimmy's focus from the plant to the driver. The farmer's grin was now so large there were smile lines etched into his forehead.

"I'm sorry," the driver almost sang out, "guess I should have given you some warning and gotten you some too. We just don't have any around our place, and spotting it today is just like getting an early present. My wife wants some to hang over the door."

"Mistletoe?" Jimmy asked.

"Yeah," he quickly answered. "You mean a teenage boy like you doesn't collect the stuff? I figured you'd have some in your pocket."

"No," Jimmy admitted, "I mean, I've heard of it in songs and stories and stuff, but just didn't know what it looked like. So you're hanging it over the door so your wife will kiss you?"

Collins laughed, "No, she'd do that anyway. We hang it because of its original meaning."

"What meaning?" a now fascinated Jimmy asked. "The only thing I ever heard was that it was meant to bring a girl and guy together for a quick smooch."

"In a way you're right," the farmer explained, "but the real story is a bit different. I can tell it if you'd like to hear it."

"Sure."

"Well," Collins began, "when the early Christian missionaries reached the Vikings, they noticed the Viking warriors viewed the mistletoe plant as having great power and mystery. It appeared they were amazed that when everything else seemingly died in the winter this plant thrived. And more than that, it grew out of what these men thought was a dead piece of wood. They attached so much significance to the power of the plant to conquer death that if two warriors met in a forest and mistletoe was overhead, they had to, by law, find a way to settle their differences without resorting to violence. Thus it became known as the plant of peace."

"That's kind of crazy," Jimmy piped in.

"Maybe," Collins agreed, "but it really gave the missionaries an opening. You see, they explained the power of faith by using the plant."

Jimmy shook his head. "I'm not following this at all. How could they use mistletoe to do that?"

Collins grinned. "That's genius at work. The missionaries explained to the Vikings that the tree growing out of the dead wood represented Christ being crucified on the cross. And, as green was the color of life for the Vikings, the missionaries then told them the ever-growing leaves represented Christ rising from the dead. And then they took it even further and explained to these men that faith, like that plant, would never desert them, remaining alive and strong even in the midst of their darkest days."

"You mean," Jimmy cut in, "like the mistletoe survives and thrives in the winter?"

"Exactly!" the driver exclaimed. "And winter was something that Vikings knew well. Their nights went on for months, so they understood what it was like to live in dark times. Their winters make ours seem like a piece of cake."

"Wow," Jimmy said while shaking his head. "But then how did it become known as the kissing plant?"

"That is just an extension of the way the missionaries used the plant," Collins continued. "You see, when these people became Christians they conducted their weddings under mistletoe to remind the bride and groom that as long as they kept Christ in the center of their lives their union would remain strong. Naturally at the end of the ceremony the bride and groom kissed, thus beginning the tradition—as we know it today. And while I appreciate this modern way of using the plant, I'm kind of sorry most folks don't realize the original meaning behind this Christmas tradition."

Collins pushed in the clutch, shifted the truck down into second, and said, "I believe you wanted to stop at Miller's, and we're almost there."

As the farmer eased to a stop in front of the store, the boy noted the streets filled with shoppers. There were old men in work clothes as well as women dressed in their finest. Kids were racing up and down the sidewalk trying to hit each other with snowballs made from snow that was rapidly melting. Farmers were gathered around the feed store smoking pipes and telling stories. There were even a few men dressed in their military uniforms lingering around the post office. The scene was like something out of a movie. It was both quaint and exciting. Noting a spray of mistletoe hanging over the store to Mabel's Beauty Shop brought a smile. Yes, it was a good day, and the warmth of the moment wrapped around him like a homemade quilt—until he saw the sign. It was strange how the two words posted on a storefront window could rock his body so hard he almost didn't hear Collins's words.

"Been a pleasure having you ride with me."

As he continued to stare at the Miller's Store sign, the boy muttered, "Thanks for the lift. I appreciate it."

"Have a merry Christmas."

"You too," Jimmy said turning his face from the sign and back to Collins.

After shaking the farmer's hand, the boy pushed the door open and stepped out of the cab and onto the street. As he slammed the door, a strange thought crept into his mind. If only he could harness the power of the mistletoe. Maybe then he could find a way to get out of his partnership with the devil and bring some kind of peace to his suddenly troubled world.

11

December 22, 1945, 1:50 p.m.

J ake, isn't that the kid?"
Sitting in the front passenger seat of a gray '34 Hudson, the leader of the trio of thieves shielded his eyes from the afternoon sun and peered through the aging car's short one-piece windshield. Like a hawk hunting a rabbit, he quickly locked onto the thin form wearing a green coat. As the hunter studied the unsuspecting prey, Jimmy focused on a store display in the showroom window at Sharp County Feed and Seed.

Simply by the way the boy moved, Jake sensed this was a much different kid than they had met in the stable. The cockiness was gone, replaced by nervousness apparent in the manner in which the kid rocked on his heels. With the Barnett kid trapped in his house and unable to be a part of the heist, Jimmy was that much more important. Obtaining that key was now critical because it made this a sure thing. There could be no more slipups. And as he studied the boy's body language, he sensed he had the kid right where he wanted him and now it was just a matter of pushing one more button. Jake rubbed his scruffy chin with his index finger and thumb, and grinned.

"Yeah, that's him. Who could miss the coat?"

Leaning forward from his position in the backseat, the tallest of the trio glanced toward Jimmy, nodded, and posed a question, "You think he's still in?"

Jake leaned back in the seat and smiled, "Martin, we got him by the throat and he knows it."

"How can you be sure?"

"I had an old con teach me when I was in stir. He taught me how to read people like a book. If you look for the right things, like twitching or even a man's posture, it says more than their words. Yeah, there's nothing like a prison education to refine your job skills."

Martin nodded, though it was likely he had no clue as to what Jake meant. Still, his eyes fixed on the boy for about twenty seconds before he asked, "You want me to get him and bring him over? After all, things have changed since that other kid messed up."

"No," Jake answered. Then, after tracing his temple with his right index finger, he added, "I don't want to draw that much attention to us. But with that Barnett kid out of the game, we do need to get the kid a message. He needs to know that we're still pulling the job." Looking over his shoulder, Jake shot out an order, "I think it's time you stretched your legs."

"OK," came the quick reply. As the thin man reached for the door handle, Jake softly barked a few final instructions.

"They probably sell candy bars in that store. Go over and buy one. Then casually stop over by the kid and give him the word to deliver the key to us tomorrow at four. Tell him we'll be parked behind the school. Shouldn't be anybody there on a Sunday. Got it?"

"Yeah," Martin shot back.

Most of the business section of Ash Flat was constructed around the turn of the century. Though only a block long, downtown had a certain regal look about it. This was due mostly to the fact that the buildings were constructed out of rock. Those thick walls gave a sense of stability that wasn't typical of a community of just a few hundred. The owners of the shops also took a sense of pride in their buildings. They kept the sidewalks swept, the wooden window frames and doors painted, and the glass clean. The community had a welcoming, friendly feel to it most felt reflected the honest values of folks tough enough to remain here during the dark days of the Depression.

Not surprisingly, crime was pretty much unknown. Though Bonnie and Clyde had once robbed a Piggy Wiggly grocery store in nearby Thayer, Missouri, the pair had steered clear of Ash Flat. In fact, the only known hoodlum to ever stroll the placid downtown street was Charles "Pretty Boy" Floyd, and he had only been a tourist.

So the locals wouldn't have expected the thin man in the bomber jacket standing in front of the gray Hudson to be anything other than a stranger stopping to do a bit of shopping. Thus, few noted Martin as he waited for Bill Evans's beat-up Model A to chug down the main drag. After smiling at Evans, the visitor ambled across the street. No one in Ash Flat would have guessed that two days before he and his friends had been casing one of the stores in their town.

As Jake watched from the car, Martin created no suspicion when he stopped in front of the feed store and glanced back toward his confederates before stepping up the three steps from the street to the raised sidewalk. Taking a deep breath, he smiled, tipped his hat to an elderly woman who was passing along the walk, pushed his hands deeply into his dirty slacks, and casually approached Jimmy. When he was shoulder to shoulder with the boy, he leaned over and whispered, "You wait right here. I've got a message for you."

The teen's eyes found Martin's, lingered there for a moment, then went back to the red pedal tractor displayed in the show-room window. Confident the kid was not going to bolt, the thin man pushed the glass and wood door open and marched over the building's well-worn pine plank floor to the main counter.

"Can I help you?" A muscular man in his mid-thirties asked.

"Yeah. Give me one of those Snickers."

The clerk, dressed in a pair of dark blue slacks and a white shirt, reached into a glass display case and pulled out a single candy bar. After setting it on the counter, he looked back to the customer. "Anything else?"

"Naw," Martin answered, dropping a twenty beside the Snickers.

The clerk shook his head and smiled, "If you don't have anything smaller, I'll have to go back and get change from the safe. I don't have enough in the register to produce $19.95. Can you wait a moment?"

"Sure."

The clerk grabbed a pen and paper from beside a gum dis-play and dropped them on the counter in front of his customer. Pointing to a box with a slit cut in the top, he said, "We have a contest to win that kid's pedal tractor we're displaying in the window. The drawing's on Christmas Eve. It doesn't cost any-thing to enter; we just need your name and address. If you're interested, just fill out the information and drop the slip into the box."

Feeling lucky, Martin nodded, picked up the pencil, and began to scrawl his John Henry on the paper. The clerk beamed, tapping his finger on the counter, before heading to the back of the store. By the time he returned, the skinny visi-tor had stuffed six pieces of paper into the box.

"Here you go: a ten, a five-spot, four ones, and ninety-five cents in coins. Good luck on the contest. Maybe you can win the tractor."

"Yeah," he laughed, "my baby brother would really go for that toy."

"Then merry Christmas to you, stranger. And come back and see us."

Martin said nothing to the clerk. After grabbing his candy bar, he turned back toward the door. He noted Jimmy shuffling from foot to foot, still looking through the glass into the store.

Stepping out into the crisp afternoon air, Martin glanced toward his friends in the Hudson as he tore open the candy wrapper then dropped the paper on the sidewalk. After taking a bite, he glanced back at Jimmy. Making sure there was no one else around, he took two steps to his left, and, without ever making eye contact with the kid, softly announced, "You meet us tomorrow at four behind the high school. Have the key."

Not turning to face the man, Jimmy whispered, "I don't know if I can. I mean, with Johnny grounded this thing doesn't look too good now."

"If you don't come," Martin answered almost sympathetically, "Jake will find you and your mom. What he'll do then won't be pretty, but either way he'll get the key. One is painless, and you get some cash. The other means you don't need to buy any presents for friends and family. You get the drift?"

"Yeah," the boy sighed.

As Martin noted Jimmy's shoulders sag, he grinned. There was something to this body language stuff. Stepping down to the street, Martin shot a final glance in the boy's direction, then nonchalantly worked his way back to the car. He'd no more than slid into the backseat than Jake pumped him for information.

"You set things up?"

"Yeah, he's scared, he wants out, but he'll show. I warned him what you'd do if he doesn't."

Jake nodded, rubbed his hands together, and grinned at the driver. "Frank, it's time we stop by the store in Agnos, pick up some grub, and head back to that stable. We really don't need to be seen around here until we pull the job."

The blocky man hit the starter, the engine sputtered and caught, and the beat-up Hudson, its tailpipe spewing blue smoke, pulled onto the main drag, made a sharp left, and eased out of town. The trio's Christmas bonus was now only a bit more than a day from being realized. With that money in hand, added to the spoils of a host of other small town gigs, they could exit Arkansas and head back to their Mississippi homes with the means to purchase any gift they wanted.

12

December 22, 1945, 2:30 p.m.

What's wrong with you?" Audrey asked. "You look like you just saw a ghost."

Jimmy quickly turned his eyes from the pedal tractor to the young woman. As he gazed down at her quizzical expression, he couldn't help wondering if she saw the fear in his eyes. If she did, she'd realize he was no better than a trapped animal.

"Jimmy, what's going on?" This time her voice was demanding, and she emphasized her question by punching an index finger into his chest. "You're hiding something, aren't you?"

Like a crook under a cop's hot light, the boy resorted to the only crutch he knew—a lie. "Nothing." The words caught in his throat enough that it barely escaped his lips.

"What do you mean, nothing?" she shot back. "You look like you're sick. I mean, really sick."

"Just Christmas," he mumbled. "I just don't like all the stuff that goes with it. You know, the shopping, presents, and silly music. Just can't wait for it to be over."

"So you don't like presents!" Audrey said, her tone now more teasing than accusing.

"Not really."

"Then I guess I should take back what I bought you."

Jimmy's eyebrows arched. "You bought me something?"

"Of course, silly," she laughed. "I needed to use my babysitting money for something. Besides, I figured if I let you know I had a present for you, you'd feel guilty and come to the church program tomorrow night."

"Ah, Audrey," he returned, shaking his head, "you know I won't do that."

"Have you bought me a present?" she demanded.

He shook his head. "I don't have any money."

"So, am I worth a present?"

"Of course," he assured her.

"And if you can give me what I wanted more than anything in the world and it wouldn't cost you a penny, would you do it?"

"Yeah," he instantly replied, not realizing he'd leaped into a trap.

"Good. I want you to come hear me sing."

Though he'd never admit it at this moment, Jimmy wanted to be there in that church more than anything in the world. It wasn't to watch Audrey either, it was to get away from an informal contract he'd agreed to without really thinking about the consequences. Now it seemed as though the only way to void that contract was unimaginable.

"Hi, kids," a friendly voice called out from the street. That voice broke into Jimmy's nightmarish concerns and brought him back to the moment. Because of whose voice it was, the moment was no more comforting.

"Hey, Sheriff Thompson." Audrey's greeting came with a huge smile. "Mary's solo in the program is incredible. I wish I had a voice like your daughter's."

Nodding, the six-foot, beefy-built Thompson stepped up from the street to the sidewalk. The glint in his eyes spelled out the pride he felt in his sixth-grade offspring, yet he wasn't going to say that on the streets of Ash Flat. That would have been bragging and the sheriff was known for his humble nature. He didn't even fudge when he talked about fish he caught. So Jimmy was hardly surprised by his reaction to Audrey's compliment.

"Miss Lankins, Mary tells me that you're the songbird in the group. I think you are her hero. So I can't wait to hear you. I just pray Mary remembers all the words to her solo. Now, I hope you two aren't up to no good!"

Those final words shook Jimmy to the core. Though logic and instinct assured him it couldn't be the case, he couldn't help but wonder if the man knew something. Maybe Johnny had tipped off his folks and they had called the sheriff. No, he wouldn't do that because then he'd be in even worse trouble. Besides, if he had, then Jimmy would be at the jail right now. So he really couldn't know anything. But was this the way it was going to be the rest of his life? Was he always going to be sensitive to everything other folks said? Would he always be looking over his shoulder?

"Phil," Mark Dietz called out from the door of the feed store.

"What's your need, Mark?" Thompson replied.

"Got something to show you," the clerk said.

"Be right there," the sheriff assured him. "Now, kids, I've got a warning for you too. Christmas is coming up, and, even though you are almost grown, someone is watching you. So you better watch out and be good at all times. Got it?"

"Sure thing," Audrey giggled.

At that same moment, a guilty Jimmy turned his eyes to the ground and nodded. That was the last thing he wanted someone to tell him. As the sheriff stepped into the store, Jimmy grabbed the young woman by the arm and whispered, "Let's get out of here."

"Sure, where? I want to look at some dresses at Miller's for my mom. Let's go there?"

"No," he snapped, his tone revealing all the apprehension he felt. The last place he wanted to visit was the store that would soon be robbed. Looking around, taking inventory of the shops in the small downtown area, he turned the opposite way and suggested, "Let's just walk for a while."

"OK," she shrugged. "Boy, you're acting strange today, even for you. You usually love to do dream shopping in Miller's. I'm kind of surprised you aren't dragging me down to look at the knife you've been wanting for years."

"Not today," he almost growled.

Ever since Martin had cornered him, his heart had been pounding at the speed of a hummingbird's wings, and his pace reflected his pulse. They were a half block from the feed store and almost to the city's only bank when Audrey yanked her arm from around his. "Slow down," she begged. "My shoes aren't made for an Olympic sprint."

Jimmy's dad had a favorite term he used when facing a situation that called for a dramatic change in attitude. He'd called it "a come to Jesus moment." Jimmy had heard him use it more than a dozen times and each marked an important moment in the elder Reed's life. Jimmy felt as though he might well be facing his first "come to Jesus moment," and how he wished his father were here to share it with him.

Just beyond the bank was a bench. In warmer weather old men would relax there and talk about times gone by. Today the regular benchwarmers were likely escaping the nip in the air by huddling around the stove inside the tractor repair shop. So, reassured that no one was in within earshot, Jimmy steered Audrey to the old wooden seat and sat down. She immediately joined him.

"What's bothering you?" she demanded as she smoothed her coat. "And don't tell me it is Christmas. It's a lot more than that."

Spreading his legs, he rested his elbows on his knees, interlocked his fingers, leaned forward, and placed his chin in his hands. As he did, he felt the girl's touch on his shoulder. It was the first time any female except his mother had delivered attention in such a comforting way. Maybe that was why the simple act drew forth an unplanned and poorly scripted confession.

"Audrey, I've really messed up big time."

He couldn't believe he'd put voice to his thoughts. What was he thinking? Actually, he wasn't thinking. Just like he hadn't been thinking when he'd agreed to be a part of the Miller Store robbery.

As Jimmy beat himself up for saying anything, Audrey allowed his words to hover in the forty-degree air for a few moments before noting, "So there is more to this than just the way you feel about Christmas."

"Yeah," he admitted, "it's more than that. To be honest, I got involved in something I can't get out of."

Leaning forward and pulling his chin off his hands and turning his face to hers, she smiled. "It's never too late to get out of something you haven't done."

Shaking his head, he pushed his eyes back toward the ground. "Not this time."

"What is going on?" she demanded. "Did your mom catch you smoking or drinking?"

"Naw," he sighed. "Besides, you know I only carry the cigarettes to look like I'm hep. And I don't drink, either."

"Kind of figured as much," she teased. "You're just attempting to look like a rebel. Too much of that Reed blood in you to really be one."

"Guess so."

Maybe that Reed blood was the problem. Maybe he'd been bred to feel guilty. After all, his grandfather had been a preacher. Maybe those morals weren't really choices, but something handed down, passed from generation to generation.

"So what is it you've done?" she asked.

"I can't tell you," he sighed. "I mean, I really can't tell you. And I haven't done it yet."

"Then," she told him, her hand once again finding his shoulder, "just don't do it."

"If only it was that easy," he answered, still not looking into the girl's eyes.

"How can it not be that easy? If you haven't done something and it's wrong, then it is easy to avoid making that mistake by not doing it. Any child knows that. You don't get in trouble for thinking about breaking curfew, you get in trouble for actually doing it."

He couldn't tell her what was going to happen. That would be stupid and draw her into the danger. Yet by simply hinting at his problem, he had opened a door that wouldn't close.

"OK," he sighed, choosing his words very carefully, "let me put it this way. I am involved in something that could get someone we know hurt. Yet if I bail, then someone else I love will be hurt."

"Broken hearts mend," she assured him, her fingers now squeezing and massaging his ever-tensing shoulder.

"It's not about broken hearts," he admitted, "but how I wish it was. It's about broken bodies."

Her fingers froze, "What?"

"I can't tell you any more than I already have, but for me to get out of this with no one hurt is going to take a miracle. And I don't mean luck here; I mean a real miracle. You see, all the pieces are moving, and I can't stop them."

"Jimmy," she said, her face and voice suddenly showing great concern and confusion.

"Audrey, it will take something much bigger than either one of us to change things. If I could have just one thing for Christmas, it would be a do-over. Sadly, do-overs only happen on the playground."

13

December 22, 1945, 2:44 p.m.

G ood to see you, Mark," the sheriff's greeting bounced off the feed store's twelve-foot walls. "How's business?"

"It's been great this year," the Army Air Corps vet answered.

"So why do you need me? Somebody shoplift something?"

Dietz shook his head as he stepped out from behind the counter. "Nothing like that. But I did get something today that you're looking for."

"If that means you've found me a present that I can give my wife, I'll owe you big time."

"Well," the clerk answered, "I do have a newfangled electric corn popper that she'd probably like. I know how good her popcorn balls are, and it might make fixing them a bit easier."

"Then show it to me," the suddenly enthusiastic Thompson replied. "I'm a pretty bad Santa. So far, I've come up dry. Well, not totally dry, I did buy Mary a couple of records she wanted. At least part of my shopping is finished. But this corn popper thing sounds like it might just help me whittle my list down to just our other two daughters."

The clerk nodded, "We've actually picked up some new customers now that we're offering kitchen appliances. The popper's over there in our home section, but that's not why I called you in. It's about a twenty dollar bill I got in earlier today."

Thompson raised his eyebrows, moving his gaze from the popper display back to Dietz. He was confused, and his eyes clearly showed it. "What do you mean, Mark? I mean, I could use a twenty, couldn't we all, but I didn't know I was looking for one."

"Remember a few weeks ago when you told me about that bored store worker in Salem who colored in Andrew Jackson's eyes and wrote his name on a short stack of twenties?"

"Sure," the sheriff replied, "he did it with a blue fountain pen. The owner of the store fired him that day. Not for doodling on the money, but doing that instead of restocking the shelves."

"And what happened a few hours later?" Dietz asked.

"After the owner closed up, that hardware store was robbed. The next day they arrested the fired clerk but had to let him go because they never found any of the stolen cash."

"What fascinated me," Dietz said with a grim smile, "was how they knew the money at his house didn't match the money stolen from the store."

"Yeah," the sheriff replied, "kind of a Sam Spade thing. The guy didn't have any of the bills he'd drawn on. In a way, he'd marked the money, and that paved the way to clear him."

Dietz pulled open a drawer under the main counter. Retrieving a bill, he handed it to the sheriff. "Phil, look at this twenty."

Thompson grabbed the money. There was nothing unusual about the back. It looked just like all the other twenties in circulation. Flipping it over clearly revealed what the clerk had spotted. Andrew Jackson's eyes were indigo blue.

"What did you tell me that clerk in Salem's name was?" Dietz asked.

"Woodrow."

"That looks like Woodrow's work to me," the clerk noted.

Thompson set the bill on the counter and pulled out his wallet. Yanking a twenty from between the leather folds, he handed it to Dietz, "This will cover your loss, I'm taking this one. Now, tell me, how'd you get this?"

"About an hour ago from a stranger—tall, thin, and shaggy—who came in here. He was kind of rough looking. Looked like it had been a few days since he'd shaved or bathed. He had on dirty pants and was wearing a pretty ragged leather Army Air Corps coat. I'd guess him to be in his twenties, with dark hair, blue eyes. That's about all I remember."

"Would you know him if you saw him again?"

"Oh, yeah," the clerk assured the sheriff. "The thing that really set me to thinking about him was I don't know many folks who look like him who are carrying around large bills. So when he produced a twenty from a wad of other twenties, it set off some alarms. I didn't have that much change up front, so I went back to the safe. It was then I noticed the artwork."

"You pilots always have such great vision," Thompson noted as he picked up the bill and slipped it into his wallet.

"You think he was the guy who pulled the job?" Dietz asked.

"Maybe," the sheriff replied. "I'm like you, it doesn't fit that a guy dressed like that would have a wad of cash. So you have reason to be suspicious. Plus, everyone in this part of the state and in southern Missouri is looking for these twenties, and last I heard none of them has shown up. What did he buy?"

"A Snickers."

"That's all?"

"Yeah, strange isn't it? He evidently didn't have anything any smaller."

Thompson glanced past the clerk to the back room. "Did this guy watch you go get change?"

"He didn't move," Dietz answered, "so he had to see where I was going."

"He might have been casing the place," the sheriff's tone was now almost muted and dead serious. "If all he wanted was a hunk of candy, he'd likely have gone to one of the filling stations or the grocery store. This smells like something rotten. Do you leave your cash in the safe overnight?"

"I have to," the clerk replied, "the bank's not open on Saturday."

"So, Mark, the weekend receipts stay here until Monday?"

"Sure do, Phil."

"Would you feel comfortable taking them home tonight?"

"I could do that," Dietz assured him.

"And leave the safe open. That way it won't get drilled or blown up." Turning back to the front door, Thompson asked, "Did you see where the guy went?"

"Yeah, he stepped out on the sidewalk and opened the candy bar. Guess I remember it so well because it made me mad when he tossed the wrapper down on the ground. When I went out to pick it up, he walked across the street and got into an old gray Hudson sedan, and a few seconds later it headed back toward 167."

The sheriff walked to the door with Dietz trailing him. When they were both on the sidewalk, Thompson crossed his arms and glanced to his right. "You said it was a Hudson. Any idea what year?"

"It was old, beat-up, and smoked when it rolled off. It was probably a '34 or '35. I didn't get a look at the nose. So, not real sure."

The sheriff smiled grimly. "Gives me something to go on, and something to give the state police too. In the meantime, I think I'll be working some overtime. Now, before I do that, what you asking for the popper?"

14

———∞∞∞———

December 22, 1945, 4:10 p.m.

M arge, when you get a second, could you come back to the office?"

Looking up from reorganizing some dress patterns that had just been scattered by Jessie Ward's six-year-old twin boys, the weary woman shook her head as she acknowledged the store-owner. What a day it had been! It seemed that, with the war over, everyone was doing up Christmas in a big way. Shoppers had come in waves, and even though it had finally slowed down there were still a half dozen folks picking over what few items were left in the gift section. This was probably just a momentary lull; the final two hours likely offered very little relief as the streets were still teeming with shoppers of all sizes and ages.

Pushing her auburn hair off her shoulder, she shook her head again and sighed. She hadn't even decorated her tree, and she was almost ready for Christmas to be over. Perhaps that was due to all her hard work at the store or maybe because the one gift she'd bought had already been unwrapped and placed on her son's shoulders. In that way, and likely so many others, she had failed James. She simply didn't have the means or the imagination to make the holidays special. Without Robert, Christmas was little more than a few minutes of awkward family interaction and an evening of pretending there was something special in the air. No wonder James didn't want anything to do with it.

The sad part was, Christmas had once held so much promise. Before the war it had been almost magical. The traditions that she and Robert had established had been meaningful. It was a joy to sing carols together and decorate the tree. Reading the Bible's story of Jesus' birth and looking out the window for Santa Claus were things they had anticipated with such great joy and delight. Even praying for snow had made it seem like the most wonderful time of the year. Yet now the wonder was gone, replaced by an emptiness she sensed would never go away.

"Marge," a heavyset woman called out from the men's clothing section, "I can watch things in the store, you go on back and see what Clark wants."

Clara Miller had come in today to help her husband. If she hadn't showed up, Marge might well have collapsed. The woman was a godsend.

"Thanks," Marge called out. "I promise I'll get right back to help you. We've got a lot of cleanup to do before we can get out of here tonight."

Moving slowly to the rear of the store, Marge entered the storeowner's small office through the half-open door. He was sitting behind an oak desk so intent on going over the day's receipts he didn't even hear her footsteps on the oak floor. Not wanting to interrupt his work, she watched him for another minute before finally clearing her throat.

"Oh, Marge," he said, pulling his glasses from his nose and setting them on top of the invoices. "I'm sorry I didn't notice you come in. I hope you haven't been standing there for too long. It's just that I'm so overwhelmed by our sales. This is the best day we've ever had!" After shaking his head and running his hand through his dark, wavy hair, he chuckled, "I may have trouble closing the safe tonight."

"Is there something you needed, sir?"

Pointing to an envelope resting on the corner of the desk, he explained, "There's something in there for you—kind of a holiday bonus. Thought I'd give it to you today in case there was anything you wanted to buy before Christmas. You're such a great worker. Clara and I appreciate you so much."

A suddenly embarrassed Marge took the gift, smiled, and clumsily stammered, "Thank you. I didn't expect anything. I was just doing my job."

"And doing it well," he cut in.

She nodded and turned to leave. Before she could clear the door, her boss's voice stopped her in the tracks.

"Oh, Marge, one more thing," Miller sang out. After she turned to face him once more, the storeowner continued, "I've been thinking about what you said about Jimmy. I really feel he just needs a man in his life right now. If it's OK with you, I want to offer him a part-time job here. Not much, you know just a few hours after school and on Saturday. With the war over, I really need the help, especially with the heavy lifting. Maybe if he's around more, I can get him to open up, and then I can kind of gently push him in the right direction. My boys turned out pretty good. So my advice must be worth something."

"That would be so great," a now gushing Marge said, and without thinking she added, "and we could use a little more money."

"Don't mention it to him," Miller all but ordered. "I want it to come from me. I'll talk to him right after the first of the year."

"Thank you." She smiled. "I can't begin to tell you how much better this makes my Christmas."

As she strolled back into the store's main room, there was a new energy in her step. For the first time in almost a year, she had a bit of hope to cling to concerning James. Maybe this would be just what he needed to get that chip off his shoulder and bring back his charming smile.

Reaching under the counter for her purse, she slipped the envelope into it. Noting it wasn't sealed, she peeked in.

"My goodness," she whispered. She couldn't believe that her employer had given her two twenties and a ten. She was simply overwhelmed. That was more than she normally made in two weeks! Pulling the cash out, she studied the crisp green bills and grinned. There was something extra here. One of the green pieces of government issued paper, one with a name written in dark ink, came with a story. A strange little man had given it to her earlier in the day. What had he bought? It was an item that cost very little, so she'd had to count out a lot of change. She glanced around the store trying to inventory what was missing from the store. The display case directly in front of her caught her eye, and then it came back to her. He'd bought a dollar pocket watch.

15

⸻

December 22, 1945, 5:05 p.m.

Jake cradled his new silver pocket watch in his palm, gently tapping the lens and smiling like a kid riding a new bike for the first time. The childlike expression remained and even grew as he held it up to his ear and listened to the instrument's rhythmic ticking. His trance only ended when a tall, thin woman, dressed in a red cotton dress, approached his table.

"You decided what you want?" Her tired delivery contained absolutely no hint of enthusiasm. In fact, it almost seemed she was hoping Jake would order nothing. If that was her wish, it was not to be granted.

"A fried ham and egg sandwich and a Coke," he mumbled. Setting the menu down, he glanced over at the two men sitting with him and added, "Get them the same."

"But Jake . . ." The gang's leader cut off Martin's argument with a wave of his left hand.

"It's simple and it's quick," the leader explained to his disappointed partner. After shaking the shiny timepiece in front of Martin's blue eyes, he added, "And we need to watch our time."

⸻

Nothing was said as the woman scribbled notes on her pad and ambled toward the back room of the combination gas station, general store, diner, and post office. When she was finally out of sight and the room was empty of all customers and staff, the third member of the gang muttered, "Wish you hadn't bought that darn watch. It's like you have to check the time every minute. What does it matter if it's one after five or four after five? It seemed we did just fine without it. There are clocks enough in store windows and gas stations to always find out what time it is."

"Martin," Jake snapped back at the tallest, thinnest member of the trio, "there's no clock in that stable. There's not even anything there to tell us what year it is. And we're holed up in that place until we do the job. Though you may not appreciate it, we are all on a schedule now. Time will be very important to us over the next twenty hours."

Staring once again at the watch's hands, Jake laughed. "You know, watching time like this is a lot more satisfying than marking time in prison. The stretch I did for breaking into the store in Mobile seemed a lot longer than eighteen months. It was as if every clock in the joint had stopped. But like I've told you guys, I learned a lot there. And what I learned has not only made us some good dough, it's kept us out of the spotlight too."

"Good dough, maybe," Frank groaned, "but there's so much more in banks and big city department stores than there is in small town stores. We're never gonna get rich this way. It's like we're nickel-and-diming our way through life."

Snapping the spring cover on his watch shut, Jake dropped it into his coat pocket. For a few moments, he ignored his partners. Pushing the chair quietly away from the table, he snuck over to the door that led to the kitchen. Glancing through a small circular window proved the woman had her back to him. She was going to be busy for at least a minute cutting some ham. Smiling, he eased out of her view to a shelf featuring thin leather gloves. He snuck a pair from the display and carefully slipped them into his coat's inner pocket. A few seconds later, he warily and silently resumed his place at the small square table.

"Those won't keep you very warm," Martin noted.

"Not meant to," Jake explained. "I just need something so I don't leave fingerprints on the door or safe. The ones I own have holes in two of the fingers. I'm not taking any chances."

"What about us?" Frank asked. "I don't want to get caught."

"I've served time," an obviously exasperated Jake explained. "Mine are on record. Has anyone ever taken either one of your prints?"

"No," the man admitted with a hint of disappointment.

"So you've got nothing to worry about. Now, who was it talking about big jobs?"

"Me!" Frank shot back. The blocky man then added, "We've been doing this small stuff for too long. We need to move up. If that store's loaded with dough, then just think what's in the bank!"

Jake grinned. This Mississippi farm boy had no clue as to the real nature of the game they were playing. To him every job was easy. He didn't appreciate how much thinking and planning went into what they hit and where.

"It's not like school," the leader softly explained, "you don't graduate from doing five and dimes and move up to First National Bank. Besides, if you'd been behind bars like I was, you'd know why we don't want to get rich. Big jobs draw big eyes. Suddenly everybody's looking for you. Never known a big-time bank robber who lived more than a few years. And all that money they grabbed, well, they spent it paying folks off for hiding places. Any cash they managed to hold onto, the cops found it after they'd blown the guys away. It's a whole lot better to be small-time, because then folks don't really pay much attention to you. Put another way, it's no fun being Dillinger. You *do* remember what happened to him, don't you?"

"So," Frank noted, his small eyes now little more than slits and his tone, while hushed, still demanding, "you learned all that in jail?"

"Yeah," Jake shot back. "I learned it from the little guys who tried to go big. The ones who taught me were the lucky ones because they didn't die from lead poisoning, if you get my drift."

Frank set his jaw and nodded while Martin shrugged.

Glancing over his shoulder to make sure the woman had not returned from the kitchen, the leader asked, "How much you got in your pockets right now?"

"More than five hundred," Martin admitted.

"And how much did you two jerks have before you teamed up with me?"

"A few bucks," Frank groaned.

"And," Jake said as he leaned forward and tapped the table, "how many times have you been shot at?"

The two looked at each other before the taller one answered, "None."

"Just remember that. You can buy what you want and no one has you in his gun sights. If you were pulling big jobs, you'd be dodging bullets everywhere you went. Oh yeah, you might be in the newspapers too. They'd be talking about you on the radio. The post office would have pictures of you. And for a little while every kid in the country might know your name, and you might even be featured in a few newsreels. Of course, you wouldn't see them because you'd be hiding out, but think of all the dough you'd have. Sounds pretty good until you realize the next step is having your coffin lowered into the ground. Now, any questions about why I pick the jobs we do?"

Frank remained mute, but Martin was obviously bothered about at least one facet of the gang's direction. Rubbing his chin, the thin man quietly posed a question that had obviously been troubling him for a while. "I got no beef about the jobs, I got more cash than I thought I'd ever have, but what about the kid?"

"What about him?" Jake asked.

"We never worked with anyone outside the three of us before. Bringing in Barnett didn't work. Now, what about this one? I mean what if either of these kids talk . . ."

"Barnett won't," Jake's matter-of-fact tone revealed his confidence. "I know his uncle. For about six months, he was on the same cell block with me. I got enough on the family that he'll keep his lip buttoned."

"But this Reed kid?" Frank offered as he joined the conversation. "How do we know he'll stay quiet?"

The leader shook his head and framed a grin so unsettling it caused a cold chill to rush into the room.

"Martin spelled things out if he didn't. The kid won't say anything because he knows we can get to his mother. I know just what she looks like. Even bought this watch from her. I'll make sure the kid hears that news again tomorrow too. I'll just pound it into his head until it turns all his dreams into nightmares."

"But," Frank argued, "that kind of thing is more out of our league than a bank job. I mean, you get the chair for doing that stuff."

"If you actually do it," Jake agreed. He let those words simmer for a moment before adding, "I wanted this job to be a snap. I scouted things out real good in Cave City, Mammoth, and even Batesville. This place looks like the easiest mark in this area and it has the greatest reward. You've seen the business they've turned in the past few days, and today they really must have raked it in. You remember how loaded with people that place was when we were in town?"

The duo nodded in agreement.

"The safe will be completely full on Sunday," Jake explained. "I've explained this a hundred times, but here it goes again. Everyone in town's going to be at the church, so the streets will be empty. I got a look at the safe when I was shopping. My tools will open it in a matter of minutes. With the key to the store in hand, we can be in and out before they've finished a third of the church program. Even if something goes wrong and it takes me longer to get into the safe, we still have a huge window of opportunity. Yet without that key getting us in the back door in the alley, it would just be too risky. Who knows who might be out window-shopping or just driving through town? But the key makes it a piece of cake. We can be out of the car and into the store in a matter of less than a minute."

"But what if the kid doesn't—"

Jake cut Frank off with a wave. "He will because he's scared. The fact that he believes we'll do something to his mother is one of our two big trump cards. When a person believes that you will kill them or someone they love, you rarely have to follow through and prove it. That's another important thing I learned in stir."

Martin looked at Phil and then back to the leader, "You said there were two trump cards?"

"Yeah, two trump cards. The other is the fact the kid's dad won the Medal of Honor. That shiny medal is our Christmas star."

"I don't follow," the thin gang member admitted.

"Didn't figure you would," Jake laughed. "In this part of the world a family name means something. This wet-behind-the-ears kid might want to grab some easy cash, but he can't let anyone know about it because that would splash some mud on what his old man did. Thus he'll keep his mouth shut even when we stiff him and don't share a cut."

Frank's small eyes showed real admiration as he posed a final question, "Did you learn that in prison too?"

"Naw," Jake grinned, "I learned that when my Daddy kicked me out of the house. It seemed he thought I sullied the Simpson name when I lifted a few items from a store in Mobile. I didn't even get caught, and it still chapped him off."

The leader reached back into his pocket and pulled out the new watch. He pushed a switch, and the cover flipped open. In the glass lens' reflection, he noted a swinging door open and the waitress appear carrying three plates and a trio of drinks. As she approached the table, he barked, "It's about time."

16

December 22, 1945, 6:10 p.m.

"Y ou about finished, Mom?"

Jimmy had been nervously wandering around Miller's Store for only fifteen minutes, but in his guilt-ridden mind it seemed more like fifteen hours. What made the time move even more slowly was it felt as though Clark Miller was watching his every move. Every time he picked up anything, from a pack of gum to a man's tie, those eyes seemed to be glued to him. Could the owner sense his guilt? Glancing into a mirror assured Jimmy that he appeared normal. If fact, if he looked anything, it was sullen. So what had triggered the owner's sudden suspicion? Maybe Johnny had talked. It would be just like him to rat Jimmy out.

"It will be another ten minutes or so," Marge yelled out from behind a stack of hatboxes. "I just need to get what we have left in stock out on the shelves for the Christmas Eve shoppers. I think it will be another big day on Monday."

There was a songlike quality in the answer and the explanation that followed that set the boy back. As he chewed on it, it dawned on him that the upbeat tone had been there since he walked into the store. What had magically erased the weariness she'd carried in her voice and worn on her face the past few days?

"James," she called out from a back corner of the large showroom.

"Yes, Mom." Turning, he tried to spot her but couldn't. She must have been behind one of the bedding displays.

"Why don't you look at some of the new clothes we have on the far wall? There are some things over there in your size. Let me know if you see something you like."

What a strange request! For as long as he could remember, she'd always told him not to let his eyes linger on things he knew the family couldn't afford. That command had even grown stronger as he had gotten older. It was like she didn't even want him to dream about buying something he really wanted. So why was she pushing him now?

As he headed to the far wall, he was forced to make a slight jog in order to step around a four-foot high, glass display case containing what was left of the store's seriously depleted stock of cosmetics. He stopped when an unusual bottle in the middle of the top shelf caught his eye. He'd seen the bottle, or at least one just like it, somewhere before. He leaned closer to read the label—*L'Heure Bleue eau de parfum*. Now he remembered. That was the stuff his mother was given as a high school graduation gift by her wealthy aunt. She loved it so much she still had the empty bottle sitting on the dresser in her bedroom. If it meant that much to her, how could she walk by this full bottle countless times each day and not want it? Moving to the other side of the glass-sided case, he cast his eyes on the price. Twenty-five dollars! Now he fully understood why no one had ever replaced the empty bottle. Who in Ash Flat could chance even holding something like that? Sammy McGloe had only asked $20 for his Model A truck!

Staring in shock at the expensive perfume caused his mind to jump into some mental calisthenics. Clark Miller had been bragging about the store's huge sales day since he'd locked the door. He'd even joked about not having room in the safe for all the cash. With Johnny now out of the picture, there would be a four-way cut in the gang's haul. That meant with his share he could easily buy his mom that bottle of L'Heure Bleue. And he wouldn't have to stop there either.

There was a five-dollar gold watch beside the perfume in that same case that would look great on her wrist. He excitedly turned his eyes to the next aisle. Not ten feet in front of him were blue dress shoes she'd probably like. Just behind that the store had a rack full of dresses that appeared to be in her size and they were a lot better looking than the old homemade ones she wore.

The thought of what he could purchase with his cut from the heist, a smile started to grow on his face, and as it did the guilt that had been eating at him began to retreat. He wouldn't spend money on himself; he'd spend it on everyone else. He'd even buy Audrey something she wanted. After all, she'd told him she'd bought a gift for him. Turning right, his eyes caught a display of seventy-eight rpm records. Audrey loved the new Perry Como hit. Placing his fingers on the top of the bin, he quickly shuffled through the choices. About halfway back, "Till the End of Time" appeared. Yeah, this was it. He could buy this number-one hit on Monday and give it to her that day. She'd be so surprised he'd thought of her.

Suddenly he felt like a big man. If he played his cards right, no one would ever know he was a part of what happened, and he could easily rationalize getting into this mess by giving all the money away. Because he wouldn't be spending any money on himself, he'd be more like a modern Robin Hood than Bonnie and Clyde. In that way it would be like admitting to God what he did was wrong without having to admit it to anyone else. And to make matters really perfect and completely clear his conscience, he'd give the church whatever he had left after buying the presents for his mom and Audrey. After all, with a few thankful prayers Rev. Jordan could wash away the stain from the bills and then use the money to help the less fortunate. Yes, this could work out pretty well after all. With a few simple acts, he could move himself from sinner to saint. Everyone in town would praise him for his incredible generosity. Even Wylie Rhoads would likely change his opinion of Jimmy.

"What are you so happy about?" Marge asked as she appeared out of nowhere and came up to stand beside her son.

"Guess I'm suddenly excited about Christmas," he answered, his smile matching hers.

"So am I," she giggled. "Mr. Miller even gave us a strand of electric lights for our tree. I can't wait to decorate it."

"I cut it this morning," he informed her, "and it is in the living room and ready for your touch. I'll even help you string the popcorn."

"That sounds wonderful," she sighed as she leaned into his arm. "You said Audrey was going to take us home tonight?"

"Yeah, she has her dad's car and she just drove up. I saw her standing outside on the sidewalk looking at the window displays."

"Hope it's not too much trouble for her."

"Naw," he assured his mother, "she's going out our way to see her grandma. They're supposed to bake cookies for the social that's taking place after tomorrow's church program."

"Well, let's not keep her waiting." Marge turned her head and looked toward the back of the store. "Goodnight, Clara. Bye, Mr. Miller. See you at church."

As they exited through the large glass-and-wood front door, Jimmy asked, "You going to church?"

"No, *we* are. Tomorrow morning we're going to walk back up those six steps and in those doors and hope lightning doesn't strike. After all, it's been a long time since we've been to a church meeting." She patted his arm, then added, "Suddenly I've got a lot to be thankful for, and I feel church is the place I need to be. I'm going to sit in that pew and count some blessings."

Jimmy nodded. Suddenly, thanks to an unexpected brainstorm, he had a few to count as well.

"I'll ride in the backseat," Marge offered. "You and Audrey can ride up front."

As his mother opened the rear door and slid in, Jimmy glanced over at Audrey. She was standing just in front of the silver Mercury's passenger fender. Leaning close, she whispered, "I've been praying you'd figure a way out of your mess."

He smiled. "Your prayers have been answered."

"Really?"

"Yeah. I've got things figured out. Everything is fine now!"

17

∞∞∞

December 22, 1945, 9:14 p.m.

E ight multicolored lights didn't cover much of the tree. In fact, they were almost completely lost behind the strings of popcorn, the ornaments, and the tinsel. Yet for Marge and Jimmy that strand of Noma electric lights made this night more special than any holiday evening since the beginning of the war. The lights were the first thing the pair hung on the tree Jimmy had cut earlier in the day. Then, after admiring them resting on the evergreen, they popped and strung popcorn and dug into the old cardboard box that held their mismatched ornaments.

"What do you think?" Marge asked as she draped a few final strands of tinsel over one of the branches.

"I think that we need some new tinsel," he laughed. "How long have you had this stuff?"

Marge stepped back to study her work, crossed her arms over her chest, and smiled. "Let me see, your father bought two boxes of tinsel in 1939. We'd made a bit more money than expected on the crops that year, so we splurged. I remember how you helped place it on the tree. While I carefully took each strand and gently dropped it into position, you grabbed about twenty and just threw them up in the air to see where they would land."

Jimmy leaned back on the couch and smiled. As he remembered that long-ago moment, a lot of other good memories crept into his mind as well. Those once-forgotten but now-remembered images drew his eyes from the tree to the guitar that was still sitting in the corner of the room. This house needed music again. How he wished he knew how to play it.

"James," Marge said, sounding as if she were announcing the kickoff to a huge event, "I think it's time we plug them in. I want to see them all lit up. Would you like to do the honors?"

Though he would never admit it, he felt like a six-year-old again. He couldn't wait to set those electric marvels aglow. Jumping up from his seat, the boy anxiously moved over to the side of the tree. As he did, a red glass reindeer hanging from a tinsel-ladled branch caught his eye. Though it had been on every family tree he could remember, he had never really examined it. One glance proved it was in pretty sad shape. Its right antlers were broken, and it was missing a hoof.

"Mom, why do you keep hanging this one? After all, it has seen better days."

"I know," she admitted, taking a few steps forward to join him by the tree. As she lightly caressed the reindeer, she smiled. It was a different kind of smile than Jimmy had ever seen. Suddenly she was not really in the present or of the moment; that smile had taken her back to a different time and a different place. In fact, it was a child's smile, not that of a grown woman.

"I take it there is a story behind it?" he prodded.

"There's a story behind everything," she sighed. "That blue ball to your left was once my grandmother Maguffee's. It was always on her tree when I was a child. The silver snowflakes were my mother's. She gave them to me not long before she died. I wish you could have known her. She made the best Christmas cookies."

"They couldn't be better than yours," he said.

"Well, I use her recipe, so you get an idea of what they were like. I still think mine don't quite measure up. Anyway, back then, when we made them, we kids always iced the cookies for her. It was a huge part of our holidays. You know, I still get hungry for her cookies each time I hang these snowflakes."

"I could go for some cookies right now," Jimmy chuckled.

"We will make some later," she assured him. Turning her attention from the tree to the front window, she asked, "Is that a car coming down our lane?"

A chill filled the room and raced up Jimmy's spine as if someone had suddenly killed the fire in their pot-bellied stove. His instincts told him who the visitors had to be. Suddenly all the feel-good rationalizations disappeared and a sense of doom quickly replaced them. The good times were over, as a frozen Jimmy got ready to face his worst nightmare.

Marge's moving toward the door threw the boy into an even deeper sense of panic. "Mom, stay where you are," he ordered.

"Why?" She was obviously shocked by his demanding tone.

"Nobody comes and sees us this time of night," he barked. "Let me get my twenty-two."

"Oh, James," she laughed, "That's not necessary. It's probably just a neighbor bringing us some fudge or something."

"Not at this time of night," he shot back. "Now stay away from that door. I'll grab my gun and go out and see who it is."

Marge's expression was a mixture of amusement and surprise. It was obvious she saw no reason to take a car driving down their lane as anything to be worried about. Still, she followed his instructions and remained where she stood, by the tree.

After pulling his gun from behind the bedroom door and making sure it was loaded, Jimmy cautiously moved to the front door and opened it about two inches. He studied the vehicle's progress as it moved by the split-rail fencing, eased past the barn, and drew closer to the house. Stepping out onto the porch and slipping into the shadows, he rested his rifle on the railing. If he needed to, he could squeeze off a shot that might at least scare them. If necessary, he might even be able to take one of the trio down, but he doubted he'd be able to stop all three. So, in a sense this was pretty much like the story of the Alamo they'd recently studied in history class: you do the damage you can do and then get overrun. He took a deep breath as he waited for the visitors to show their hand. Were they going to separate and surround the house or just march up to the front door and barge in? For the life of him he couldn't figure out which would be better.

Crouching by the railing, he studied the car as it slowed to a stop, its brakes squealing and its rear lights glowing brighter. A scant few heartbeats after easing into the parking spot, the driver switched off the motor and then the lights. With clouds covering the sky and no lights in the yard, it was now as dark as a tomb.

Jimmy was so scared he could barely breathe. He was sure the unexpected visitors, though still in the car, could hear his heart pounding a hole in his chest. It was beating loud enough that the vehicle was likely rocking.

Get out, he silently pleaded. Let's just get this thing over.

A few seconds after his unvoiced request, the driver's door opened and a lone figure stepped out. Jimmy couldn't see enough detail to make out who it was, but the fact that the other two were staying in the car was a good sign. For at least a few moments it would be a one-on-one battle. With no hesitation, the visitor moved through the grass toward the porch. As the visitor grew closer, Jimmy's hand tightened on the trigger. He waited for the figure to mount the first step before his unsteady voice issued a cold demand: "Don't move, and get your hands in the air."

"If I do that, I'll drop the cookies."

"Audrey?" he stammered, a rush of relief flooding his body.

"You were expecting Santa?" she quipped, climbing the final two steps to the porch.

"No," he laughed, "Santa only visits good boys. Mr. Rhoads will tell you I haven't been good this year."

Leaning the rifle against the porch railing, Jimmy stepped over to his guest and, with a wave of relief evident in his now steady voice, announced, "You're just in time to help us plug in the lights on the tree."

18

December 22, 1945, 10:10 p.m.

O h, Audrey," Marge laughed, "I can't imagine your grandmother dealing with a raccoon."

The girl's eyes flashed like Independence Day fireworks as
she continued her story. "You should have been there. One
of us must have left the backdoor ajar. We looked around
and the creature was not just in the kitchen, he was on the
table helping himself to the cookies we had just decorated.
Grandma spit out a few words I didn't know she knew and
grabbed her broom. Her first swing caught the coon on the
side of the head, but he didn't move. Instead he lifted up on
his back legs and glared at us. He looked like a small bear
wearing a burglar's mask."

"That must have been scary," Marge said.

"Not really," the girl explained, "he didn't look mad, just
aggravated. It was as if he was saying, 'How dare you strike me!'
It was when she whacked him the second time that all heck
broke loose. He grabbed a cookie in his mouth, jumped off the
table, knocking cookies and a sack of flour to the floor, and
made a mad dash right for us. He actually ran right between

Grandma's legs and then scrambled up her Christmas tree, knocking off ornaments as he climbed. A half dozen glass balls must have broken as they bounced off the limbs and hit the floor. When he got to the top, he grabbed the angel, clenching the cookie between his teeth, and hung on for dear life. It was then Grandma made like Babe Ruth and got ready to swing again.

"This time she really put her full force behind her effort. She missed the coon but knocked the tree with a broadside that brought it crashing to the floor. Ornaments were bouncing, tinsel was flying, and the animal was once again on the floor. Grandma was raising her arms to try one more sweeping swing when the raccoon sprang from the branches and back into the kitchen. About five feet from the door he stopped, whirled, and looked at both of us as if we were possessed. For at least thirty seconds, with Grandma still holding the broom over her head, no one moved. Then, in a flash, the coon, the cookie still in his mouth, spun and raced out the door."

"He didn't drop the cookie?" an astonished Marge asked.

"Nope," Audrey replied, "but when he got out the door, Grandma moved faster than I've ever seen her move and snapped the lock into place. After taking a huge breath, we looked around at the mess and starting laughing. We laughed 'til we cried, and then, after wiping our tears, we started to clean things up. It took about thirty minutes to get the tree back up. We also found at least a dozen cookies on the floor."

Jimmy looked at the plate the girl was still holding in her hands. When she noticed his expression, she grinned, "No, these are not those cookies. I made this batch after the animal left. But what is funny is Grandma gathered up the ones from the floor and went to the back door and tossed them out. She told me if the animal wanted them that badly he might as well have some to take home to his family."

After the laughter had died down and the cookies were placed on the table, Jimmy glanced back at the tree. It was then he realized his mother hadn't finished the story she'd begun before Audrey had unexpectedly arrived. "Mom, what about the reindeer?"

"Oh, you don't want to hear that now."

"Yes, I do, and I bet Audrey would as well. Tell us where the red reindeer came from."

After their guest nodded her agreement, Marge stepped across the room and back to the tree. As she stared at the ornament, the childlike expression once again framed her face. Never taking her eyes off the red reindeer, she picked up her story.

"My grandmother might have never gone hand-to-hand and face-to-face with a raccoon, but she was a pretty special lady. Every year at Christmas she gave each of us grandkids a glass ornament. I was six when she died, so I got six different ones. Three of them fell off the tree and shattered when I was a kid. I lost a fourth one, a tiny bluebird, the Christmas before James was born. This reindeer is one of two I have left that connect me to that special woman."

Jimmy's eyes wandered over the tree. Where was the other one? The only glass ornament he saw was the reindeer. Stepping closer, he continued to search the branches, but no glass object appeared in his view. "Mom, I don't see the other one."

"It's not on the tree," she explained.

"Why not?" Audrey asked. "It is too delicate? Are you afraid it might get broken?"

"No, not at all. I used to put it up every year. It's a yellow star, and it once sat on top of the tree."

Jimmy's and Audrey's gaze went to the empty point at the tree's summit. There was nothing there now except for an empty branch, reaching for the ceiling, looking very barren.

"Why haven't you put Dad's medal up?" Jimmy asked, his eyes falling back to his mother. "I mean, that's where you always put it."

"I don't know," she whispered. "I'm torn on if I want to put that medal or the glass star up this year. If it is all right with you, I may wait until Christmas Eve to make that decision."

"Sure, Mom."

Jimmy shook his head; so the medal was now starting to create convoluted feelings for his mother as well. Maybe the sadness had finally overcome her sense of pride in having her husband die a hero. Maybe it now reminded her of their great loss too. Maybe, just like it did for him, that government-issued star now meant loneliness and pain.

As Jimmy and Marge continued to study the empty spot at the top of the tree, an awkward silence fell over the room. Beyond the crackling of the logs in the stove, there was no sound. It was Audrey, pointing to the end table, who finally broke the sober mood.

"What's that? It's really beautiful!"

Grateful to be concentrating on anything other than the Medal of Honor, Jimmy explained, "Oh, Calvin Jenkins carved that for me. It's a candlestick."

The girl picked up the gift and studied the intricate carvings in the wood. As she did, Marge retreated to the kitchen and pulled a red candle from a drawer. She was returning to the living room when Audrey tilted the wood piece and saw something she'd missed.

"There's something written here. It's a Bible verse—Matthew 25:35-40."

Of course, Calvin had told him that if Jimmy read that verse he could understand why Calvin took the time to visit with and give gifts to those others ignored or had forgotten. Yet, thanks to his own worries about the mess he'd gotten himself into, he hadn't even thought to look at the base and find those verses.

"Put this in it," Marge handed their guest the candle. "And Jimmy, once she gets it set, you light it."

A few seconds later the simple act of striking a match and lighting a wick dramatically changed the mood of the room. After Audrey set the special gift back on the end table, each of them silently admired the candle's warm glow.

"I kind of feel like Martin Luther," Audrey sighed happily.

"What do you mean?" Jimmy asked.

"That's where lights on the tree started," the girl replied. "Luther saw the stars in the sky and then thought of the light that came into a dark world when Jesus was born. When he got home, he tied a candle to their Christmas tree and that is where it all began."

"And you know what that reminds me of?" Jimmy chimed in.

"What?" Marge asked.

"We haven't plugged in our new electric lights yet."

In unison, they all turned to the tree. As the two women looked on, Jimmy moved back to the tree and grabbed the cord. He was stretching it toward the wall plug when his mother's voice stopped him.

"Wait, let me turn out all the house lights."

A few seconds later only the red candle lit the room. Eight small lights soon joined its warm glow. Two were green, two were blue, another two were yellow, and the final two were red. They filled only a small portion of the tree. But those eight, combined with the candle on the table, seemed to bring a light to the holidays that Jimmy had not experienced in years. As Calvin's candleholder said, they brought hope. But now, as he basked in the glow of the holiday illumination, he wondered if the path he'd chosen to unburden his conscience wasn't really just another way of trying to bury a wrong. Maybe he didn't have things figured out after all.

19

———

December 23, 1945, 12:07 a.m.

*T*he happy laughter and lively conversation left with
Audrey. Alone again, Jimmy and his mother sat on opposite ends of the couch silently staring at the tree. Finally, just
after midnight, Marge, after reminding Jimmy that Clark and
Clara Miller would be picking them up for church at ten-thirty
sharp, got up and went to her bedroom. After she closed the
door, Jimmy flipped on the room's only lamp, which sat beside
the couch, and blew out the candle.

Just six hours ago he'd been so sure he'd found a way out of
the mess he'd willingly plunged into, but now that exit seemed
to be littered with landmines. It started with the downfall of
his dreams of being Santa Claus. He couldn't really buy anything with the money. If he did, people would put two and two
together and know where he got the cash. As he had no logi-
cal explanation that would satisfy a first grader, much less his
mother, Mr. Miller, or the sheriff, he would have to confess.
So his cut of the take was worthless. Anything he used, no
matter how small, would point a finger of guilt in his direc-

tion. Yet not being able to use even his part of the loot solved nothing.

Looking across the room, he noted his mother's gray purse. As much as he didn't want to, he had to get into that bag. Now was as good a time as any. Slipping his shoes off his feet, he tiptoed over to the other side of the room. There, sitting atop a dark wooden bookshelf was what he needed. No, it wasn't actually what he needed; it was what he had to have. After glancing over his shoulder to make sure her door was still shut, he slowly pushed the clasp and the bag opened. Tilting it toward the lamp, he studied the contents. There were a few loose tissues, a tube of lipstick, a compact, a black billfold that had once belonged to his father, and a pencil. At the bottom was also a keychain. He didn't need that, as those two keys were for the house and the barn. It was a single key on the other side of the bag he had to get. Pinching it between his fingers, he retrieved the metal object and slipped it into his pocket. Taking a deep breath, he snapped the bag shut and returned to the couch. When he gave the key to Jake tomorrow, his job would be over. At least he hoped it would. Surely they wouldn't want him there when they blew the safe or whatever they did to get the money.

Leaning back into the cushion, his eyes found the eight-by-ten black-and-white photo hanging on the far wall. It was a picture of his father in his Marine dress uniform. Jimmy had studied that photo a hundred times—no, a thousand times—but tonight it seemed different. Tonight that picture seemed to be studying him. In a panic, his eyes darted back to the purse. The picture had seen it all. It had observed his actions. That picture could also see right through him to the larceny and guilt in his heart.

Jimmy tried to calm his jitters. What he was thinking was stupid. That picture was nothing more than paper. It was just a captured moment in time. Then an even more frightening thought hit him. It wasn't the picture; it was his dad who knew. But wasn't that impossible? His father was dead. The dead had no senses, no feelings, no emotions. So they couldn't feel, and if they couldn't feel then Jimmy couldn't let his father down. Maybe before the war he could have, but not now. So why was it suddenly bothering him? Why was it eating at his gut? Why wouldn't it leave him alone?

He looked back at the wall. It still felt as though the picture was staring at him. Jimmy fought the urge to run over and tear it from its place. If he did, how would he explain that to his mother? No, it had to stay there, and he had to get the thought out of his mind that his dad was watching him.

Grasping at straws to wipe the strange thoughts from his mind, Jimmy turned his attention to the first thing he saw—the candleholder. He almost choked as he lifted it from the table. After all, the message Calvin had so carefully carved into the wood was so far removed from the reality of Jimmy's life. Where was the hope? About the only place he saw it was carved into the wood.

Hope—it was just a word. There was no power in it. In fact, it was really nothing more than a grown-up word for "wish." You hope for this, you wish for that, they were really the same thing. A kid said "wish" and an older person said "hope," but saying it did nothing. Even believing it as you said it didn't work.

How many times had he hoped his dad was alive? It had to be at least a hundred, and not one of those hopes or wishes had come true. And prayers, what were they but voiced hopes? He'd prayed for his dad too, and that hadn't done any good either. Calvin was wrong about *hope*. There was no power in the word, only disappointment.

Now, *light* was different. That he could understand. There was light and darkness, and he had slowly found the darkness a bit more comforting than the light. In fact, he had grown to love the night because it hid the stark reminders of the reality of the day. So, while providing hope wasn't an option, the candle actually served a purpose: it provided some light. If the power went off during a storm, it could be put to good use.

Jimmy reached out and traced the contours of the wooden object. Calvin was indeed talented. This was the work of a true craftsman. Perhaps if he had been born in a different place and into a different set of circumstances, he could have been a sculptor. People might have paid large amounts of money for the works of Calvin Jenkins. Except, how could you be sure you actually had one of the artist's works? After all, he didn't sign them—or did he?

Grabbing the candleholder and flipping it over revealed a signature of sorts, but it wasn't a name. As he was feeling too on edge to sleep, maybe finding that verse would give him something to think about, other than Jake and his gang and a photograph that seemed to know what was in his mind and on his heart.

"Matthew 25:35-40."

He whispered the words a few times before setting the candleholder back on the table, getting up, and moving back to the bookshelf. The third book from the right, just past a copy of *Tom Sawyer*, was a black-covered Bible. Easing it from its spot, he returned to his customary place on the couch. Plopping down, he leafed through the first few pages until he found the table of contents.

Jimmy couldn't remember reading the Bible, so he had no idea where Matthew was. He didn't even know if it was in the Old or New Testament. He ran his finger down the chapter listings one by one until he finally found the book he needed.

Matthew began on page 781. He quickly thumbed through the thin printed and bound pages until he discovered the right one. He then slowed and, after wetting his finger, flipped a few more pages until he got to the chapter he needed. Once again using his finger as a guide, he searched verse by verse until he found the thirty-fifth. He was surprised the verses he was looking for had been underlined in pencil. Had his father done this, and if so, why? He glanced back at the photo on the wall. It still seemed to be watching him. Returning his gaze to the Bible, he began to read. As he did, his eyes darted from word to word and his lips silently moved.

> For I was an hungred, and ye gave me meat: I was thirsty, and ye gave me drink: I was a stranger, and ye took me in:
> Naked, and ye clothed me: I was sick, and ye visited me: I was in prison, and ye came unto me.
> Then shall the righteous answer him, saying, Lord, when saw we thee an hungred, and fed thee? or thirsty, and gave thee drink?
> When saw we thee a stranger, and took thee in? or naked, and clothed thee?
> Or when saw we thee sick, or in prison, and came unto thee?
> And the King shall answer and say unto them, Verily I say unto you, Inasmuch as ye have done it unto one of the least of these my brethren, ye have done it unto me.

After he finished, he set the book to one side. If these verses said what he thought they said and meant what he thought they meant, he now had a better understanding of what Calvin was doing and why those actions made him feel as if he was hugging God. Then something else hit him: maybe his father had underlined this verse when he had helped Calvin through the bus driver's worst days. But even if he had, what did all of this mean to him? After all, he was a fatherless son. He had little money and no real hope. He was a prisoner to his situation. As he saw it, he and his mother were the least of these. They had literally become that when his father had died. So folks should be helping them.

Noting a box of matches on the end table, he opened it, retrieved a match, struck it against the side of the box, and held the lit match to the candle's wick. After the flame took hold, he shook the match out, put it back on the table, and studied the candle's glow. Hope and light, those were the things Calvin had said he wanted to give people at Christmas. Yet how could Jimmy have those things in his life? What would it take for him to know either of them this year?

Looking back at his father's picture, Jimmy shook his head and whispered, "I've messed up, Dad. You'd be disappointed in me. But there's not really any way out. When you left, you told me to take care of Mom. I can't go back on that, so I have to go through with helping Jake and his gang pull the job. I'm so sorry. Just wish you were here, because maybe you could show me a way to somehow fix all of this mess. Still, if you hadn't died, I wouldn't have done it. So, it's kind of your fault. You decided to be a hero, living out those verses I just read—well, that really created the mess I'm in."

The picture didn't answer. He didn't really expect it to. The miracles that happened inside the Bible's pages—those stories his father had told him so long ago—didn't happen anymore. This was the era when you made your bed and you were stuck lying in it.

Jimmy snapped the Bible shut, stood, and slowly made his way back across the room. Bending to a knee, he began to slip the book back into its spot. It was just as the Bible touched the shelf that he saw it. There was an envelope sticking out of the Bible as if marking a place. How had he missed it? Perhaps opening the book had caused it to shift. Jimmy eased down to the floor, crossed his legs, set the book in his lap, and opened the book to the spot. A quick glance told him the envelope had been inserted in the Book of Luke where the Bible presented the story about Christ's birth. It was the very story they used to read from this very same Bible when Jimmy pushed the nativity scene figures from one place to another. Yet it was not the memories of those long-past holidays that now grabbed him, it was the writing on the envelope.

"To Jimmy from Dad, to be opened on Christmas Eve, 1942."

Why hide it in the Bible? Why didn't he just give it to his mother and let her give it to him? Jimmy didn't puzzle for too long before logic kicked in. His Dad figured they would continue to read the Christmas story each year. So they would find this note just in time for his first Christmas away from them. But his mom never did read the Christmas story after he died. In fact, she'd never again even opened his Bible. When she read, she used her own.

Now the overpowering question became, should he open the envelope?

In truth, there was no reason not to. In fact, it was overdue. But a troubling feeling ate at him. What was in it? It felt like nothing more than a letter. What if the words in that letter brought even more guilt than he was already feeling? Perhaps it would be better just to forget it or maybe even throw it away.

Jimmy finally retrieved the letter from where it had been hidden for more than three years, closed the Bible, and put it back on the shelf. Getting up, he moved back across the room, blew out the candle, unplugged the Christmas lights, and switched off the lamp. Retreating to his small, ten-by-ten bedroom, he sat in the dark on a quilt that was likely fifty years old, a quilt that his father had slept under as a boy, and ran his fingers over the edge of the envelope. He had to make a decision. Finally, after more than five minutes of thought, he opened a drawer in the nightstand and slipped the letter into a place that hid a few old baseball cards, a high school annual, and a picture Audrey had given him last year.

He pulled back a curtain and stared out into the darkness. He was more comfortable in the dark. It was the midnight hour that gave him the cover he needed to be something other than what a Reed was supposed to be. So it wasn't time to let the light reveal what his father had wanted him to know three years ago. In fact, that time had long since passed. Whatever his father had written was meant for a much younger boy, one who wasn't facing the problems Jimmy now faced. Just like his dad, those times and those words were now dead.

20

———❊———

December 23, 1945, 9:00 a.m.

D
o you think it's really OK to rob a place so close to Christmas?"

That question had come completely out of left field. After taking a bite of a cracker, Jake looked across the stable at Martin and shook his head. "What difference does it matter when you pull a job?"

"I don't know," the suddenly nervous man stammered, "it never has bothered me in the past, but I had a dream last night."

"A dream?" Jake grinned. After tossing a half a cracker to the floor, he laughed. "You're having dreams now? Well, tell us about it. Anything that makes you worry about the easiest job we have ever pulled has got to be good."

Martin pulled his tattered leather Army air jacket closer to him, leaned back on the bench, and stabbed his heel in the building's dirt floor. "It's nothing."

"No," Frank teased, "tell us about it."

Reaching down and picking up a piece of straw, Martin drew in the dirt for a second and then, after taking a hard

———❊———

swallow, began his story, "I just dreamed that someone was telling me to go home."

"Go home?" Jake queried. "You mean like Mississippi and that one-horse town you were raised in or do you mean that goat farm your daddy runs?"

"I don't know," the man replied, glancing at the floor. "I didn't really understand where it was. But I swear this voice was telling me to drop everything I was doing and go home. I got to thinking, maybe my mom's sick or maybe it's one of my brothers or sisters. Anyway, it's like someone was warning me. The voice didn't make it sound like I had an option either. It was like go home now or something bad was going to happen."

"Wait a few hours," Jake laughed, "and we'll all go home together."

Martin pushed himself off the bench and ambled over to the door. He opened it slightly and looked out at the Arkansas hills. The trees were leafless, the sky was nickel gray, and the wind was cold. As the strong breeze cut into his cheekbones, he shivered. Allowing the door to close, he turned back to the others. Both sets of eyes were following his every move.

"I got just over six hundred bucks," he explained. "That's really all I need. In fact, I never dreamed I'd have this much money at one time. I want to get home with this six hundred. I need to do that. I know that's just what I need to do!"

"You're going to go home with a lot more than that," Frank argued. "You've just got to wait a little while longer."

"No," Martin sighed. "I don't want any more. You guys take it and keep it. Live it up!"

Jake slowly got up, deliberately moved to the suddenly unsteady member of his group and jabbed a finger into the taller man's chest. "You're going to let a little nightmare stop you from your biggest payday ever? That dream was probably nothing more than a bad piece of ham stirring up your innards."

"No!" Martin argued, "My grandma had dreams. She said it was sometimes a curse and sometimes a gift, but when she had them she paid attention and so did we. Saved us from a tornado once too. Another time we found some buried money thanks to her dreams."

Jake grinned. "You've gone soft, boy. You need to go over there, sit down, open a can of Vienna sausage, and get your wits about you."

"No, Jake. Not this time. I'm hitting the road. I'll hitch a ride over to Hardy, jump on a freight train, and head south. You don't need me on this gig—with that key you could do it all by yourself."

"You're yellow!" Frank shouted.

His accusation echoed off the walls and caused all three men to freeze. For an instant, no one even breathed.

"Maybe," Martin admitted. "But I just got a feeling that I'm closer to getting—what was it you called it—yeah, to catching lead poisoning. I feel like a turkey in a hunter's gun sight, and it's not a good feeling. I'll just grab my bag out of the car and take off."

Without warning, Frank leapt from the bench, his beady eyes showing rage and contempt and his fist clenched in anger. "You won't walk out on us. I won't let you." Charging like a mad bull, the stocky man lowered his shoulder and knocked Martin through the door. They rolled on the wet ground until Frank got his bearings, drew back his right arm, and landed a fist on his friend's face. As he did, Martin's head bounced back and hit a jagged rock protruding up four inches out of the red clay.

Seething with anger, Frank pushed himself up off the ground and hovered over the now limp body, "Get up and fight, you coward. If you want to leave us now, it will be over my dead body."

Jake, who had been standing in the door, casually strolled over to the still ranting Frank. He patted the big man on the back and suggested, "You need to control that short fuse. You're getting worked up over nothing."

Frank, his face twisted and still huffing like a Frisco Line locomotive, looked over at Jake. "What?"

"Let him go," the leader softly said. "He's not going to talk. If he does, he'll be in the same trouble we are. Besides, he's right, we'll have a lot more for us if the cut is just two ways. Now let's get him off the ground. We've even got plenty of time to drive him to the train tracks."

Dropping to one knee, Jake slapped Martin's face a couple of times and watched for a response. When nothing happened, Jake touched the still man's cheek. He held it there a second and shook his head. Patting Martin's coat, he reached into the right front pocket and yanked out a roll of bills. He smiled grimly as he pulled himself upright.

A confused Frank looked on, as Jake counted the cash. "Six hundred and thirty dollars! That means three hundred and ten for you and three-twenty for me. After all, I deserve the extra ten for counting it." He peeled off the announced amount, handed it to Frank, and took the rest and stuffed it into his own coat pocket. Looking out at the gray sky, he shrugged, "Well, his dream was right, he's gone home."

"What?" Frank whispered.

Showing no emotion, Jake muttered, "Just a two-way cut now. Pick him up and let's hide him under the old straw in the stable. It'll be weeks before someone finds him, and by then no one will connect him to us."

"I killed him?" Frank moaned.

"Yeah, you did. Or maybe there's just something to this dream business. I guess he should have had that dream the night before last. Then he might be back at that goat farm now."

Jake pulled his watch out of his pocket and snapped it open. Even if Martin was out of time, there was still plenty of time to do what he and Frank had to do.

21

December 23, 1945, 9:47 a.m.

*P*hil Thompson dropped his wife and daughters off at church for Sunday school before heading down to the sheriff's office. Though he usually sat in on Lloyd Glass's men's class, he felt something far more important pulling at him today. He wanted to make a few calls to see if there was any news on the gray Hudson. Finding out who owned that car might well lead him to the person who had pulled the Salem robbery.

Thompson was unlocking his office door when a yellow Ford coupe pulled up and Mark Dietz jumped out. The sheriff waited at the entry, leaning up against the frame, to see what his friend wanted.

"Morning, Phil."

"Merry Christmas! You on your way to church?"

The feed store owner shook his head. "No, not much of a churchgoer. I just wanted to catch you and visit about what we talked about the other day. Did you find out anything about the car?"

"So far nothing, but I'm just going in and making some calls to check if anything has come in since last night. Why?"

"Well," Dietz explained, "I realized after I went home that the guy who gave me the bill filled out some slips for our drawing for that toy pedal tractor. So I drove into town and went through the entries this morning."

"There have to be hundreds of pieces of paper in that box," Thompson noted. "I mean, if you didn't get a name how can you know which one is that guy's?"

Dietz smiled and suggested, "Let's step inside out of this brisk wind and I'll show you."

Thompson flipped the light on in a sparse office containing a desk, three wooden chairs, a coat rack, and a file cabinet. On the gray walls hung a few wanted posters, some local rules and regulations, and notices of tax meetings. On the six-by-four-foot oak desk was a candlestick phone, an ashtray, a note pad, a few pencils, and a state highway manual. Moving to the edge of the desk, Dietz pulled about a dozen pieces of paper from his pocket and dropped them beside the note pad. The sheriff leaned over the other man's shoulder as he arranged them.

"OK, Phil, we have three names here; Jackie Price, Sam Kellog, and Martin Crane."

Moving closer to the desk, Thompson nodded and then posed a question, "You had a lot more names than this in that box. I must have filled out a dozen entries myself."

"Yeah," Dietz admitted, "you filled out twenty-two. I knew who those other people were because they were either regular customers, route drivers who bring me supplies, or locals who heard about the contest and signed up. These three are the only strangers who entered. So one of them has to be the guy who had the twenty taken from the robbery in Salem."

The sheriff leaned over and studied the slips. The names and addresses were on each of them. Price listed a Mountain Home, Arkansas, address as his home. One quick call would provide the information he needed on him. Kellog was evidently from Bolivar, Missouri. That meant some digging with folks he didn't know. It was therefore likely he wouldn't be able to get anything until sometime tomorrow or maybe even after Christmas. The third name listed North Andover, Mississippi, as a home address. It might take a few calls to get any information on that one as well. Still, this at least gave him something concrete to pass along to the state police.

"Good job, Mark, this will surely help. It'd mean a lot to those boys up in Fulton County if we could hand them their suspect as a Christmas present."

"That's not all," Dietz chuckled. "I can narrow it a lot further. I figured out which one of these three is the guy who passed the twenty."

"How?" Thompson begged. "Are you psychic now? Did they teach you that in flight school?"

"No. It's nothing like that. It has more to do with the contest being so popular. When I started this giveaway, I attached a string to a ballpoint pen and tied it to the box. Well, so many people signed up that the pen ran out of blue ink. I was about to replace it when this guy walked in and asked for a candy bar. Anyway, the pen I gave him had black ink. After he left, I attached a blue ink pen to the string and all the other entries have been written in blue. So this Martin Crane is your guy. You get me a picture of him, and I'll identify him."

"Good job," Thompson laughed as he picked up one of the entries. "Let me keep this one and put the rest back in the box."

"Including Crane's other ones?"

"Yeah," the sheriff explained, "he might just be innocent, and if he is then he deserves a chance to win your tractor."

Thompson watched Dietz gather up the slips and walk out the door before he picked up the phone. After talking to three operators, he finally was connected to the county office that handled law enforcement for North Andover, Mississippi. He was surprised when someone actually answered his call.

"Deputy Finch, can I help you?"

"Deputy, this is Sheriff Phil Thompson from Ash Flat, Arkansas. I'm trying to find somebody from North Andover named Martin Crane. Just wonder if you've heard of him?"

"Yeah, what's he done?"

"So," Thompson replied, "he's got a record?"

"No," Finch answered, "but he's been flirting with one for the past year."

"Is he average height, kind of thin, and looks a bit scruffy?"

"Yeah, that describes him to a T. He's not real bright either. High school dropout, got kicked out of the service, so he's kind of a worthless son of a gun. Haven't seen him in a month or more. His folks own a farm maybe six miles out of town."

Thompson puzzled on the information for a moment. "Does he drive an old gray Hudson?"

"Not while he was around here. His folks were poor, and he usually rode a mule into town. It's gray, but don't think it was named Hudson."

Thompson forced a laugh before asking, "Deputy, do you know if he runs around with anyone?"

"There's a guy, in his late twenties, name is Frank Pelton. I used to see them together a lot. Pelton is a powerfully built guy, maybe a bit overweight, about five foot six, and has small eyes. We've had him locked up for drunk and disorderly a few times, but nothing serious enough to take prints or make him pose for a picture. And before you ask, he doesn't own a car either. What have they done?"

"I don't know if they've done anything," Thompson explained, "but Crane passed a twenty dollar bill to one of our merchants that was part of a store robbery over in a town not far from here. If he shows back up in your area, could you let me know?"

"Sure, I'll put the word out. Who do I call?"

"Sharp County, Arkansas, Sheriff's Office and ask for me, Phil Thompson."

Thompson set the bell-shaped receiver back into the cradle. He felt a bit better about the situation now. He had a name, and he might even have a great deal more too. If this guy was the one who pulled the job in Salem, then he might just be hitting the feed store this weekend. Maybe he was casing it out when he dropped the bill. If that proved true, he was sure glad he'd told Dietz to take the store's money home.

22

———⊗⊗⊗———

December 23, 1945, 10:50 a.m.

*F*our hours and forty-five minutes. That was how long it was
until Jimmy passed the key to Jake. On a day when little
kids seemed to think time had slowed to a stop, for Jimmy it
was moving at the rate of the military's new jet planes. Those
precious minutes that separated him from seemingly innocent
teenage mischief to grown-up crime gnawed at him like a
hungry dog going after a meaty bone. In fact, the meeting was
all he could think about.

Beyond a simple, "Good morning," he hadn't spoken on the
trip to church. That was all right, as his mother had talked
enough for both of them. He had been forced to mumble a few
holiday greetings as he walked from the parking lot and up the
church steps, but at least no one had tried to engage him in
real conversation. Once they entered the sanctuary, someone
finally approached who was not going to let him off the hook.

"Mr. Reed."

Jimmy stopped in his tracks. He'd forgotten that Wylie
Rhoads went to this church until they were literally toe-to-
toe.

———⊗⊗⊗———

"Good to see you at church, son."

Jimmy nodded. "Good to be here, sir."

The superintendent studied the boy for a moment, then added, "Judging by the fact you're here this morning, I'm thinking you might just be planning a turnaround. Back in the days when you came here every week, you were a top student and not any trouble at school. This is a good move for you."

"Thank you, sir," he replied. "Believe me when I say I sure don't want to get in trouble anymore. I've made some mistakes that I hope to never make again."

"So you've seen the light," Rhoads said with a smile.

"Yeah," Jimmy assured him, "I've seen the light."

The school administrator patted the boy on the shoulder. "Christmas is a good time for light. Enjoy the holidays."

As Rhoads walked over to the right side of the church, Marge pushed Jimmy to the left. She steered him toward an empty spot in the third pew from the back before asking, "What was that all about?"

"Nothing important," Jimmy whispered. "He just wanted to know how things were going."

"Glad to see you two are getting along," she said quietly after they sat down. "You need him in your corner."

"I know," Jimmy agreed. "I plan on doing what I need to do at school to keep him happy. That will be my present to you and him."

She patted his hand and smiled. "I couldn't ask for anything more."

At this point neither could he. But coming back to the good side after crossing the tracks to bad was not easy. In fact, it might be impossible. As he glanced over toward the far side of the room, he noted a large wall clock, and it made him feel like a condemned man. It was as if the clock was rushing to the hour when his life would be forever changed. If only there was some way to get out of this mess without having his mom hurt.

Somewhere in the background, deeply hidden from his consciousness, he barely heard a piano playing holiday carols, but even though they were all familiar, he didn't really recognize them. As the clock's hands seemed to speed up with each second, Jimmy lost track of those entering the old red brick building and filling the fifty-two pews. For the moment, there was only the clock.

"Look at June Bailey," his mother whispered, her eyes pulling his from the clock and pushing him to look toward a fifteen-year-old strawberry-haired girl sitting with her mother on the far right side of the church. "She has grown to be a beautiful young woman. That green dress is just perfect on her."

Jimmy nodded. During this entire school year, he'd noticed the changes in June, all the boys had, but for the moment those changes meant nothing to him.

Reaching into his pants pocket, he fingered a small key. This was the key to his future. It would be the instrument that not only unlocked the door to Miller's Store, but would also spring the latch on the door leading to a life that was far afield from what those who knew him best felt he was destined to live. It was this tiny brass-colored key that would sully the name he'd been born with and probably tarnish the medal his father had earned.

Jimmy was so focused on the nightmare his life had become he didn't catch the music director's cue to stand. So the congregation was already on the second line of "Away in a Manger" before he stumbled on his feet. As he mumbled, "lay down his sweet head," he noticed Audrey in the choir. When their eyes met, she winked. She still believed his problems were behind him. He could tell by her look she thought he'd figure a way out. She couldn't have guessed that after she left their house last night he'd realized there was no exit. The path he had chosen was one that had only one destination and there would be no turns onto side roads named Hope.

It finally dawned on him that he was not going to be able to sit through church if he didn't change his focus. He had to think of something else. His eyes wandered through the crowd and the first person they locked onto was the last person he wanted to see. There was Sheriff Thompson sitting with his family. The star pinned to his suit jacket reflected the light from a nearby window. That shining star squeezed the breath from Jimmy's lungs. The sheriff had to suspect something, at least that was what the dark side of Jimmy's brain argued. If he didn't, then why yesterday's strange warning?

His throat dry, Jimmy's eyes darted across the aisle. There was Clark Miller, and worse yet, he was looking his way. There was something funny about the way the storeowner had talked in the car. He kept turning the conversation back to his record sales day and how much money was in the safe. It was as though he was tempting Jimmy to try to get it. Did he know something? Could he read the plan in the boy's eyes?

The job had yet to be pulled, and Jimmy felt as though he were running for his life. So he certainly didn't want to see anyone in a position of authority, not this morning or maybe not ever again.

Moving his eyes to the right, he found a somewhat less judgmental face. There was Calvin, and it was the first time Jimmy had ever seen him in a suit. It might have been old and ill-fitting, but it was a suit. Yet he still looked like a farmer. For the first time all morning Jimmy smiled; not even being dressed up could hide that rural look on Calvin's deeply wrinkled brow. The sun had taken its toll and had aged him even more than his years.

As he scanned the rest of the congregation, he saw almost everyone he knew, including Miss Masie, the schoolteacher he had met with Calvin. Yet there were others obviously missing; Joe and Marie Foster weren't there. As he chewed on that fact, he wondered if there was a church in the area for black folks. He'd have never thought about that before. Maybe he wasn't the only one trapped by circumstances that were beyond his control. Just as he started to feel a bit better, he realized his trouble was due to a choice he'd made; the Fosters hadn't made a bad choice. The nation just wasn't ready to accept them yet. Until this very moment, the line drawn between the races had never bothered him, but now the walls built between people due to skin color hit him as hard as a left hook from a heavyweight champion.

As Jimmy thought more deeply about the unfair nature of life, he glanced back at those singing about goodwill to men. Was he the only one here to notice this? Then his eyes found the bus driver. Calvin understood and in his own way he was doing something about it. What would the man do for Jimmy if things blew up? Would he come see him in jail?

Jimmy's dark thoughts plunged him into an even deeper depression until twenty minutes into the service, when a solitary movement drew his attention. It was Audrey moving from her spot in the choir and over to the pulpit. Wearing a red dress with green buttons, she looked like a holiday dream. As he stared at her, Jimmy felt his heart squeeze a bit tighter. Maybe for the first time he realized this classmate, this girl he'd known all his life, was more than just another friend. She was the person who never quit believing in him. She buoyed his spirit, and her steadfast belief suddenly made him feel even more unworthy. The key in his pocket proved he was so very different from Audrey. He was sure she would lose all faith in him if she ever found out what he would be doing later today.

Squirming in his seat, Jimmy once again fingered the key that had changed everything. As he did, Audrey cleared her voice and spoke.

"The song I'm about to sing," she explained to the packed church, "was written by a Frenchman about a century ago. Recently I was surprised to discover it was brought to America in the 1850s, not as a Christmas song, but by an abolitionist. Why? Because its lyrics clearly stated it was against Christian nature for anyone to own another human being. In the third verse of 'O Holy Night,' you will hear me sing the words that echoed in the hearts of those who believed slavery was not just wrong, but was a sin."

She paused a moment before softly adding, "I didn't think about that until recently. I was on a vacation and noted several highly decorated black men in Army uniforms. They had flown planes in the war. They were called Tuskegee Airmen. These men couldn't even drink from the same water fountain as I did. In these days, when so many of all colors fought to keep America free, I want to read these lines from 'O Holy Night' so that we can hear the message Christ shared."

> Truly He taught us to love one another;
> His law is love and His Gospel is peace.
> Chains shall He break for the slave is our brother
> And in His name all oppression shall cease.

Audrey took a breath and looked Jimmy's way. He forced a smile and nodded his head. Like Calvin, she got it. She understood, and unlike him, she grasped the concept before she did something stupid.

"Today," she continued, her eyes not leaving Jimmy's, "we need to embrace those who are different, while at the same time we should recognize that our choices can make us slaves as well. The key to not being a slave in this world or of this world is the hope found in faith."

Jimmy's eyes dropped to the floor. She had said it. The key was hope. Why hadn't she told him that last week? Why hadn't Calvin shared the stories about his father sooner? If he'd just known!

Audrey's rendition of the carol left several, including Marge, in tears. It seemed her clear voice had brought heaven to earth and had delivered the wonder of Christmas in all its majesty to Ash Flat, Arkansas. In truth, the service should have ended right there, but it didn't. After Audrey had given her testimony in song, the postmaster Vince Evans read the Christmas story from Luke, and then the congregation stood and sang "O Little Town of Bethlehem" and "Go Tell It on the Mountain." Finally, the Rev. Jordan stood up and delivered his message. By the looks of those packing the small building, the clergyman had fashioned a winner. But Jimmy couldn't have known—he was too busy praying for a miracle that he felt he didn't deserve or couldn't happen. Even as he voiced a silent amen, he knew he was a slave to a decision he'd made. There simply wasn't a miracle big enough to free him. So, while God came and visited the rest of those gathered that morning, Jimmy felt so far removed from Him, he might have been in another room with the doors locked by the key he carried in his pocket.

23

⁂

December 23, 1945, Noon

While Marge hovered in the foyer visiting with friends, Jimmy pushed through the crowd and hurried down the steps. He stopped only to button his new coat and turn up the collar before heading out toward the Miller's black Buick. He was halfway to the old sedan when he heard Audrey's voice calling out to him.

"Jimmy Reed, slow down!"

He turned, a sense of shame etched on his face and panic raging in his gut, and watched warily as she strolled toward him. She was not alone. Beside her was a man he'd never seen. He was probably around forty, slightly built, about five feet ten, and might have weighed one fifty. He had light eyes that could only be called Carolina blue. As striking and unusual as they were, they were deep, warm, and friendly and framed by smile lines as he grinned.

"You must be Jimmy," he said as he approached. The four words were easy to understand, but the accent was like none the boy had ever heard. It wasn't really British, but it shared

143

something with those from England, even though the only Englishmen he'd heard were on the radio.

"Young Mr. Reed," the man almost shouted as he stuck out his hand, "I've come a long way to meet you. In fact, I've traveled halfway around the world."

An unsure Jimmy took his hand. The man's grip was firm, giving a hint of a person much stronger than he appeared.

"Where are you from?" Jimmy asked the visitor as he released the grip.

The man held his answer as he studied the boy's face. His smile, which already covered the bottom half of his face, grew even larger. After seemingly completing an inventory of every individual feature between Jimmy's forehead and his chin, he answered, "New Zealand."

As the boy mentally spun a globe trying to remember where New Zealand fit onto the world map, Audrey jumped back into the conversation, "Mr. Buck was at my house when I got home last night. He'd contacted Dad because he was looking for you. I told him you and your mom would be in church this morning. Anyway, my mom is telling your mother about him right now, and that's why you will be coming to our house for lunch."

What was this all about? What business did this man have with him? Then a horrifying thought hit, making the skin on the back of his neck stand up all the way to his scalp. Did this have something to with the gang? A shaken Jimmy turned from Audrey to the visitor and asked for an answer that scared him down to his bones, "You were looking for me?"

"Yep," Buck replied, "my name is Kevin Buck. I knew your father back in '43. I met him in the Philippines."

An uncomfortable silence seized the moment as Jimmy shoved his hands into his coat pocket and again studied the person standing in front of him. Thank goodness this wasn't about the pending store robbery. Besides, why would a man from the other side of the globe be concerned about that? Yet even as the boy drew a deep sigh of relief, something almost as troubling crept into his head. This guy was either crazy or shell-shocked or maybe a bit of both. After all, you can't meet someone after they have died.

Now it was Jimmy's turn to study Buck. There were no obvious signs of mental problems, but wasn't that always the case with these types? They seemed normal until they spoke and then it became apparent they were mentally ill. At least that was the way Ella Simpkins was. The old woman looked and acted like an old maid schoolteacher until she opened her mouth and told stories about people who she'd just talked to. Only those friends had been dead for years. So the best route was to defuse the bomb before it went off. As carefully as he could, Jimmy delivered the truth.

"I'm sorry, Mr. Buck, you must have me confused with someone else. Doesn't surprise me. Robert Reed and Jimmy Reed are both pretty common names, and this is a big country. So you just have the wrong town and the wrong Jimmy."

"No," Buck assured him, that smile still running from ear to ear, "I have the right young bloke. You're the lad I came to see."

The deluded but happy man was standing firm. Gently pushing him to confront the truth wasn't going to be easy. Yet, as this would dredge up old memories that would hurt his mother, this charade couldn't continue.

"I don't mean to seem rude," Jimmy softly argued, "but you said you met Dad in 1943. My dad died in '42. He won a Medal of Honor holding off Japs in April of that year. He manned a machine gun so a lot of Americans could escape. We have the documentation to prove it."

"Didn't know about the medal, but I know the story well," Buck assured him. "I heard it from your father's own lips."

"You're serious?" Jimmy whispered. It couldn't be true. He had to get that through Buck's head. "I'm sorry, sir, but the truth doesn't lie. We have the official records."

"Did the Marines tell you they saw him die?" Buck asked.

Jimmy thought back to that day so long ago. The visitors had told the story of his father refusing to leave and manning the machine gun while a bunch of men loaded into a plane and got into the air. They talked about his staying at his post even as several more planes loaded up and took off. But in that story nowhere did they mention an eyewitness report of his being shot.

"This has got to be a joke," Jimmy insisted.

The answer was immediate, "We Kiwis might be known for our sense of humor, but, mate, I wouldn't try to yank your string on this one. I can assure you that I'm serious as I can be. Let me show you something."

The visitor pulled an envelope from the Bible he'd been clasping and handed it to Jimmy. "Open it. Take a look at the picture."

Jimmy studied the white envelope. There was nothing written on the outside, and it wasn't sealed. Pushing back the flap, he peeked inside. The complete contents appeared to be a single three-by-five-inch black-and-white image. Jimmy shifted his gaze back to the visitor, who nodded and smiled.

"Look at it, Jimmy," Audrey urged him.

He didn't fully understand why, but a sense of dread seeped into his heart and sank down to his gut, and it didn't stop moving until it had weakened his knees. It was just a picture, but that picture might well rewrite history—maybe not world history, but at least his own.

"Jimmy," Audrey pleaded, "I saw it last night after I got home from visiting you all. You need to see it too."

Pinching the photo between the index finger and thumb on his right hand, the boy slowly extracted it from its hiding place. On the back was a date—April 4, 1943. Flipping it over revealed the image. The man on the right, dressed in khaki pants and a white shirt, was obviously Kevin Buck. The other person, wearing a ragged Marine uniform, was incredibly thin and months overdue for a haircut. A shaggy beard covered his gaunt face. In a way he looked like no one Jimmy had ever seen before—that is, until he gazed into the eyes. Those eyes were the same ones that had stared at him from the photo on the wall last night. Those eyes belonged to his father!

Jimmy didn't so much voice as mouth, "How?"

"That was taken in the spring of 1943," Buck said. Stepping closer, he pointed to the picture and explained, "As a part of my job, I had a camera with me. I gave it to a native, explained how to use it, and he took this snap of the two of us."

"Snap?" Audrey asked.

"Sorry," Buck laughed. "That's what we Kiwis call a photograph."

"I don't understand," Jimmy softly said as he continued to stare at the image.

"This is not the place to go into that," Buck answered. "Too much noise and way too cold. I'll tell you all about it over lunch. I understand we're having turkey. I'm looking forward to trying it."

Buck reached over and patted the boy on the shoulder before stepping past him and moving toward the Lankins' car. As the visitor moved away, a shocked Jimmy looked again at the photo. It was his father. It couldn't be anyone else, but it was still impossible.

"You OK?" Audrey asked, moving closer to his side.

"Don't know," he replied. "This is way too weird."

"But it's true," she assured him. Slipping her arm under his, she asked, "I know it's cold, but do you want to walk the two blocks over to our house?"

"Yeah," he sighed. "I need a bit of time to clear my head."

24

December 23, 1945, 12:32 p.m.

N ow you too?" Jake was so angry he was screaming. "Did you have a dream?"

Frank shook his head as he leaned against the old Hudson, "No, but it's different now. Martin was my friend. I'd known him for years."

"And you killed him," Jake hissed.

"Didn't mean to," the stocky man replied. "I just didn't want him to leave."

"It may have been an accident," Jake admitted, his voice now a bit calmer, "but that wouldn't matter in court. You charged him and knocked him to the ground, and he died. It was your fist that did the damage; it drove his head into that rock. That's at least murder two and might even be murder one!"

Jerking his thick arms over his fleshy face, Frank moaned, "I didn't mean to do it. I swear I didn't."

Jake shook his head in disgust as the other man sobbed. Turning away from the scene, he glanced over the landscape. They'd parked the car off a dirt road that led down to the

Strawberry River. The fast-moving stream reflected the deep gray sky and together they emphasized the chill that still hung in the air.

"It's going to snow," Jake said to no one in particular. It was if he'd suddenly gained the gift of prophecy: the words had no more escaped his lips than a lonely flake floated toward him. A half dozen more quickly followed it. In a matter of minutes, the snow was steady. If it kept this up, there would be a couple of inches on the ground by nightfall.

Reaching into his pocket, Jake pulled out his watch. Flipping it open, he checked the time. It was just over three hours until they had to meet the kid. Dropping the timepiece back into its place, he asked, "What do you want to do, Frank?"

"I want to go home," came the immediate reply.

Turning back to his lone remaining partner, Jake shook his head. "I'm disappointed in you, boy. You're looking at the biggest haul we've ever made, and you want to walk away."

"Well, it just doesn't feel right now."

"You mean now that you've killed someone?"

Tears once more began to flow from Frank's small, beady eyes. They ran down his square cheeks and dropped to the red clay. "You can do the job on your own," he sobbed, sitting down on the car's running board.

"Yeah," Jake sighed, "I can. And if necessary I will. So what are you going to do?"

"I want to catch a freight home," he affirmed. "I want to get out of this place and see my folks for Christmas. I want to try to forget what I've done and find some way to make it right."

"You want a miracle," Jake laughed. "You're never going to forget that punch or carrying Martin back to the stable and covering him with straw. That's going to haunt you the rest of your life."

Frank nodded. "I know. I wish I'd never gotten involved in this mess." Reaching into his pocket, he yanked out several hundred dollars in bills and tossed them onto the ground.

"Yeah," Jake snapped, "that's going to make everything better."

"It's dirty money," Frank moaned.

"No." Jake grinned, reaching down to pick up what his partner had just thrown away. "There's nothing dirty about the money—you're the one that's dirty. You're the one with blood on his hands. You're soft. And just think: you were the one wanting to know why I didn't set us up with a bank job."

Staring out into the falling snow, Frank shook his head. At this point, he was no use to anybody. The man who a day before had wanted to jump into a big job now didn't have the stomach to knock over a small-town store.

After picking up the cash from the ground and stuffing it into his own pocket, Jake posed a question, "You want me to take you down to the tracks?"

"Yeah," the man sighed. "I want to go home."

"You ever going to talk about what happened?"

Frank turned and stared in disbelief at the ex-con. "Are you kidding? You think I'd admit to killing someone? You think I'd ever tell anyone what I've done today? I just want to forget it and pretend I never did anything with you. I'm going to pretend like we never met at that backwoods bar."

"No, I don't guess you would spit out what you know. So I'll tell you what I'll do. You hang out here for a couple of hours with me, then I'll drop you off around the railroad tracks in Hardy."

"So you're still pulling the job?" Frank asked.

"Of course. I'm not going to spoil my Christmas just because you suddenly grew a conscience. There's nothing on this earth that can keep me away from that dough. The picking is easy, and now I'm not sharing it with anyone."

25

‒‒‒∞∞∞‒‒‒

December 23, 1945, 12:45 p.m.

There were many in Sharp County who labeled Joan Lankins as the best cook in the region. Her dishes had won more ribbons at the county fair than any person in history. The feast she had prepared for this special Sunday before Christmas dinner featured some of her best work. Beyond the turkey, there was her special dressing, mashed potatoes, green beans, canned homegrown corn, whipped butter, and homemade white bread still hot from the oven. Yet, while the mouthwatering delights at most of her meals captured all the attention, today they ran a poor second place. The story woven by the man from New Zealand was all those gathered around the table could think about.

"So, Mr. Buck," Marge said, her voice so hushed everyone at the table had to lean forward to hear her, "you're telling me that Robert survived that battle in the Philippines?"

"He was wounded and captured," Buck explained. "He was then placed in a pen or maybe a better description would be a makeshift stockade with a bunch of Filipinos. His injuries were not severe and one of the local men who had been locked up with him was a doctor. So patching him up was easy."

"If he was in prison," Audrey asked, "how did he escape?"

Buck leaned back in the wooden chair and rested his head against the wall's green and yellow floral-print wallpaper. "It seems the Japs were much more concerned with going after fleeing Marines than they were dealing with the locals. They must have somehow forgotten there was an American Marine locked up with the Filipinos. So the security around the pen was pretty lax. On the second night five of the men escaped and Bob was with them."

Jeff Lankins was a well-built man in his late forties. A banker by trade, he cut wood for fun and because of that his body was as rock hard as a coal miner. Blessed with a quick smile and large brown eyes, the only thing deeper than his intellect was his curiosity. Thus, Buck's story had drawn him in like a moth to a flame. After wiping his mouth with a cloth napkin and tossing it on his now clean plate, the banker posed a question. "How did Robert avoid getting picked up again? I've read that there were tens of thousands of Japanese soldiers in that area."

"And," Buck added, "they were after any man who didn't look like them. But as Robert had been tossed in with locals rather than other Americans, he was literally forgotten about. It was those locals he escaped with who smuggled him into the jungles and safety."

The visitor took a deep breath, patted his stomach, and looked over at Joan, "Mrs. Lankins, your meal was amazing. How I wish my wife could cook like this."

"Thank you, Mr. Buck," she said, smiling. "I would be happy to share my recipes with you. I could write them out and send them back with you to New Zealand."

Pushing forward, Audrey didn't allow the man to follow up on the offer. "So it was the Filipinos who took care of him."

"Yeah, they got him well away from the main Japanese forces. That's where I found him, or maybe I should say that's where he found me. I was on the run as well. I was an engineer working in the Philippines when the war broke out. I had some local men who worked for the same company I did, and they hustled me away just as the invasion happened. I was safe for a while, but in late March my luck ran out. A small group of Jap soldiers happened on the house I was staying in. They weren't too friendly, and they pushed me around a bit."

"Pushed you around?" Jimmy cut in. "What do you mean by that?"

"I guess a better way of saying it is they literally beat me nearly to death. It seemed they thought I might know something, and I didn't. They locked me in a house—a shack, really. That's when your father and about a half dozen Filipino men showed up. They snuck into the camp that night, did what they had to do, grabbed me, and spirited me off to a cave. A few weeks later, after some pork and rice and a lot of sleep, I was pretty much my old self."

"What was Robert doing?" Marge asked.

"He was fighting the war in his own way," Buck quickly replied. "Where we were was on the coast. If we climbed the mountain behind the cave that served as our house and headquarters, we could see the ocean and study the movement of the Japanese ships. Bob would watch, then write down the information, even taking pictures with my camera, and the locals would take this information to a Catholic priest in the village about ten miles away. The clergyman had a hidden radio behind the altar and would transmit the information to our friends in Australia."

"Wow!" Mr. Lankins exclaimed. "This sounds like something out of a Hollywood film."

"But that's not all he did," Buck continued, "he also led local church services, which we held in the cave, and he took care of orphans and widows. He even formed a little school and was teaching kids how to speak English."

"So he's alive?" a disbelieving Jimmy asked.

There was a hush around the table as five sets of eyes locked onto the visitor. As Buck considered the question, his smile evaporated. It was replaced by a grim look that quickly dashed any hope that had been growing over the past few minutes.

"No, Jimmy," the Kiwi sighed. "His luck ran out on Christmas Day, 1943. Someone must have tipped off the Japanese about us, or maybe they just got lucky. We were singing carols when the bombers flew in. They went after the village. During the attack your dad rounded up about a dozen kids and took them to the cave. That was the last time I saw him. A bomb hit near me and knocked me about forty feet into the jungle. When I came to my senses, it was several hours later and the village was in ruins. I worked my way up to the cave, but the bombs had blown away enough of the mountain to collapse the entrance. A few of us tried to dig it out, but you couldn't do it by hand because there were tons of earth where the entrance had been. It would've taken heavy machinery weeks to move it. I can't begin to tell you how hopeless I felt.

"That night I sat alone at that spot just outside where the cave entrance had been and looked up in the sky. There above me was the brightest star I'd ever seen. Don't know why, but that star gave me some hope. I don't know if you all realize it, but *hope* is a pretty powerful word. It can drive a man, even someone like me who was all alone, to keep fighting to live. Knowing I couldn't stay where I was, I started walking west, following that star. A few days later a band of Filipino soldiers found me and got me back to my people.

"I later told an American medical officer my story. He promised me he'd turn things over to military records. Therefore I'm a bit surprised you didn't know this. But maybe he lost track of the report and it fell through the cracks."

As each person digested this new information, the room grew silent. Buck's dramatic narrative was that overwhelming! It had not just changed a timeline, it had added chapters onto a life story. For Jimmy, it was not easy coming to grips with the startling fact that his father had died much later than he had believed. He had picked up the photo of Buck and his father and was again studying it when his mother found her voice.

"So, Mr. Buck, why did you travel halfway around the world to see us? You could have written us and shared this story."

"It was a promise I made to Bob," he explained. "I told him that if I got out and he didn't, I'd go to the States and visit some of the places he talked about so much. He also wanted me to meet Jimmy. I had to wait until the war ended and I was out of the service, but here I am."

Buck gazed at the boy for a moment. "He told me you were the finest young man in Ash Flat. He was very proud of you and had such confidence in what you were going to become."

The words should have brought great pride, but instead they stung. Avoiding the eyes of everyone at the table, Jimmy tossed the picture on the table, pushed his chair back, and quickly left the room. Grabbing his coat from a living room chair, he rushed through a front room, out the door, and down the steps. Marching quickly out to the street, he only stopped when a combination of falling snow and tears clouded his vision. As he wiped them away with his sleeve, he heard a soft voice call out behind him.

"You all right?"

Turning, he looked into Audrey's sweet face. He shook his head.

"Kind of like losing your dad twice," she whispered. "Got to be tough."

"It's not that," he sighed.

If only he could tell her the truth. But while that might ease his guilt, it would place her in danger. He wouldn't do that.

"What is it then?"

"I'm not the person Dad believed I was."

Audrey put her hand on his cheek and smiled. "You were that person when he left, and you can be that person again. His hopes for you can still be realized. It's not too late."

There was that word again. Why was it so easy for everyone else to claim when hope was so elusive for him?

"Look at that snow, Jimmy. We're going to have a white Christmas."

"I don't need a white Christmas," he sighed, "I need a miracle."

His fingers found the key in his pocket. As he turned toward the school, the image of a ticking clock once again filled his head. It was now less than three hours before his life forever changed!

26

⚬⚬⚬

December 23, 1945, 3:55 p.m.

Though a series of bizarre things had created a temporary sense of havoc, really things were now playing out much better than he'd planned. Jake Simpson had figured he'd have to cut this deal three ways, but thanks to a partner's unexpected death and the guilt that death created in his other partner, now it was just winner take all. And on top of that, he'd gotten all the cash Frank and Martin had left. Yes, it was a shame that Martin had died, but Jake felt no remorse in having his and Frank's loot in his pocket. The big man had stupidly thrown it away, and the dead man had no use for it. That was the reason Jake never allowed himself to mourn over situations or people. What happened just happened, and all he did was try to figure a way to turn what happened to his advantage.

As his vacuum windshield wipers slowly brushed the heavy snow from his windshield, he pushed the Hudson steadily but slowly along the highway and toward Ash Flat. He was absolutely alone for the first time in months, and it felt good. There was a peace that came with solitude, and it was something he hadn't experienced when keeping company with his two confederates. As he listened to the steady hum of the six-cylinder motor, he smiled. In spite of the unexpected events of the past few hours, everything had still come together, and the moment of the big payoff was drawing closer with each swipe of those wiper blades. In just a few hours he'd be heading southeast with more cash in his pocket than he'd ever had. Best of all, he was sure that he would leave no trail to follow. After all, Martin couldn't talk, Frank was headed out of state, and the kid wouldn't say a word, and that made this, along with the other small-town robberies he had pulled, the perfect job.

As he passed by the Ash Flat city limits sign, he reached into his pocket. With one hand on the steering wheel he punched open the pocket watch cover. It was three before the hour. Two minutes later, with the big wet flakes now so thick he could only see about fifty feet in front of him, he found the dirt road leading to the school. As he pulled behind the large, rock building he saw a lone figure. The kid was standing beside a wall, using it to shield him from the blowing snow.

Jake set the brake but didn't turn off the motor. Opening the door, he stepped out into the increasingly inhospitable environment. He took in the scene, carefully checking to see if anyone else was there to witness the meeting, before flipping his coat collar up against his neck and tramping through four inches of fresh snow.

"Where's your friends?" Jimmy asked as the two stood face-to-face.

A sly grin crossed the man's face. "I decided I didn't want to cut this thing three ways."

As he considered the cryptic reply, Jimmy nervously mumbled, "What did you do to them?" His tone indicated he really didn't want to know.

"Same thing I'll do to you and your mother if you don't have that key," Jake shot back. "It's cold out here and I don't want to freeze to death, you got it?"

"Yeah."

"Let's see it, then."

The kid hesitated, turning his face toward the east. As he did, the wind suddenly died to the point you could almost hear the snow hitting the school's slightly sloping roof.

"What's that?" Jake asked, his ears pulling his attention in the direction the boy was looking.

"It's the choir practicing. They're having an extra rehearsal before they perform tonight."

Jake noted the strains of "Angels We Have Heard on High" drifting across the snow. The next time they sang that tune, he'd be inside the store helping himself to maybe a thousand in cash. Now, that was a tune he couldn't wait to hear again. As the wind picked up, muffling the strains coming from the church, he threw his attention back to the kid.

"Enough stalling," Jake barked. "Let's have it."

"You can't do this," Jimmy softly argued.

"What?" Jake demanded, stepping even closer to the boy. Now there were just inches separating them.

"You can't do it. It's Christmas, and as wrong as stealing is any other time of the year you just can't do it now. It's really not right this time of the year."

Jake leaned over so that he was looking directly into the boy's green eyes. "According to that church over there, it's not right anytime, so pulling a job at Christmas is no different than pulling it on the Fourth of July. This is just another day for me, and it stands to be a very profitable day too."

He grabbed Jimmy's collar and yanked him so that they were nose to nose. "Listen, kid, you were pretty cocky in that stable. You didn't back down at all. You were ready for the payoff. I don't care if you are standing ankle deep in snow, this is not the time to get cold feet. Do you get my drift?"

Jimmy reluctantly nodded, reached into his pocket, and a few seconds later produced the key. He stared at it for a moment before handing it over. Jake pinched it between his thumb and finger, smiled, and asked, "You sure this is the one?"

"I know the key," Jimmy assured him. "I picked it out of my mom's purse last night. It's the one she uses to let herself in the store each morning."

"Front or back door?"

"It works on both."

"Great," Jake said, grinning. "Get in the car."

"What?"

"You heard me, get in the car."

"Hey," Jimmy argued, a bit of fire showing in his voice, "I came through, I gave you the key. I've done my part, and I don't even want a cut."

"You're not getting a cut, kid, but you're also not leaving my sight until I get the money and head out of town. After I'm free and clear, I'll drop you off. But if somehow I do get caught, I want a local with me to face the music. If we have to sing, I want it to be a duet!"

It was obvious Jake had caught Jimmy by surprise as the color instantly drained from the kid's face. He was like a fox in a wire trap; there was no way out. But just like the animal, the kid was going to try to make a break. Jake anticipated that and was ready for it.

Jimmy pushed his back from the wall and cut right, but he made it only three feet before Jake tripped him, sending him tumbling to the ground. As he struggled to his feet, the man reached back and delivered a sweeping right hook to the kid's left cheek. The blow knocked Jimmy back against the wall before he slid down the building into the snow.

Jake hovered over him for a few minutes, grinning. "Get up and get in the car, or I'll just beat on you some more. And by now you've figured out you're no match for me."

After wiping a bit of blood from his mouth with his sleeve, Jimmy awkwardly stood. Brushing the snow from his coat and pants, he moved toward the Hudson. He'd made five steps when another car pulled down the alley and stopped. Jimmy and Jake froze as the driver's door of the flathead Ford opened and a man stepped out.

"Jimmy Reed! Is that you down there?"

The kid grinned, "Sure is, Calvin."

"I thought I recognized that green coat."

"Who is that?" Jake whispered as the visitor walked toward them.

"The school bus driver," Jimmy shot back.

"Don't say anything," Jake demanded.

"Jimmy," Calvin said as he closed the distance between them to less than ten feet, "what are you doing out in this blizzard? I thought you and your mom were staying over at the Lankinses' until tonight's service."

"I was just taking a walk in the snow," the boy answered.

"Too cold out here for that nonsense," the chilled man said, his teeth chattering. Calvin then looked past the boy to Jake. "Howdy."

"Hello."

"Anything I can do for you?" Calvin asked.

"No," Jake replied. "I was lost and saw the kid walking, so I stopped to ask for directions. He was able to give me what I wanted."

"Jimmy's a good kid like that," the bus driver replied. He studied the stranger for a second and then turned to Jimmy. "You need a ride back to the Lankinses' house?"

"Yeah," Jimmy enthusiastically replied, "that'd be great."

Without another word, the now freed Jimmy marched through the fresh snow toward Calvin's car. As he happily moved away, Jake tried to come up with some reason to pull him back, but he found nothing that wouldn't throw suspicion on him. Like it or not, he was going to have to let the kid go.

"You need anything else?" Calvin asked.

"No," Jake assured him. "The kid gave me all I needed."

"Roads are kind of bad," the bus driver explained. "You might want to hole up here for a while. There's a program over at the Methodist church at six; you'd be welcome there. Even going to have some food afterwards."

"No, thanks. I'm used to driving on the snow. I've got some chains if I need them. I'll just be on my way in a few minutes."

"Be careful," Calvin said as he turned and headed toward his sedan.

Jake's eyes never left the man until he got into his car and drove off. So much for using the kid as a lookout, but with the snow and the church program, there probably wasn't a need for one anyway. Now that he had the key, this job would be easy.

Opening his fist, he looked at the shiny metal object resting in his palm. Tonight, during the singing of old carols in a small village, one pretty smart guy from the East—well, the Southeast—was going to reverse the old tradition of bringing gifts. Instead, this visitor would take some.

Dropping the key into his pocket, Jake pulled out his watch. In just two hours, his plans would be realized.

27

———⊙∞⊙———

December 23, 1945, 4:15 p.m.

S trange that guy should be lost," Calvin noted as they
pulled away.

Jimmy was so relieved to be free, he almost didn't hear
Calvin. The only thing worse than being trapped into giving
Jake the key would have been being there when the place was
robbed. At least now, he'd be at the church. With his mom
there too, they both should be safe.

Evidently growing tired of Jimmy not answering his question, the driver rephrased it. This time his tone demanded a
response, "Didn't you think that guy's story sounded strange?"

"No!" Jimmy quickly answered. "Maybe he just has a poor
sense of direction or didn't have a map."

"Something just doesn't feel right," Calvin argued as they
passed the church and turned right toward the Lankins' home.
"Maybe it was his tone, but something about that situation got
under my skin."

"What do you mean?" Jimmy asked.

Calvin replied, "Why would a guy who was lost stop
behind the school on a day when there aren't any classes? It

———⊙∞⊙———

just doesn't make sense. He'd have a better chance of tracking down someone for directions by sticking to the highway or just pulling into a drive and knocking on someone's door."

"Guess he saw me out walking." Jimmy realized the excuse was lame the moment he spit it from his lips.

The joke had always been that Calvin Jenkins was part bloodhound. When he got his nose to the ground, he didn't look up until he found what he wanted. So what could throw him onto another trail?

"With this heavy snow," Calvin now sounded as though he was thinking out loud as he spoke, "he'd have to have gotten off the main road to see you walking. I've got a gut feeling he's up to no good. I think after I drop you off I'm going to talk to Sheriff Thompson. If the guy hasn't left town, he might want to talk to him."

There was no doubt Jake looked and sounded suspicious. A man needing directions would not have turned off 167 or pulled behind the school. And while he didn't want Miller's Store to be robbed, Jimmy also couldn't afford to have the sheriff find his mom's key on Jake. So what story could he dream up that Calvin would buy? As he reflected on his options, the hound literally smelled blood.

"Jimmy," Calvin noted, "your lip's bleeding."

Jimmy brought his hand up to his mouth and touched it. How did he explain this? He couldn't let the driver know the stranger had decked him, but in this case there was not really any other excuse he could logically toss out except maybe his own clumsiness. "It's nothing. I just fell on an icy patch of ground."

Calvin nodded but said nothing. He remained mute until he pulled the Ford up in front of the Lankinses' two-story frame house. As he pushed the car into neutral, he turned to face his passenger. His normally happy face now looked more like that of a sad circus clown.

"Thanks for the ride," Jimmy said while reaching for the door handle. He gripped it tightly as he added, "I appreciate it. I didn't realize just how cold it was."

Calvin nodded to acknowledge Jimmy, but he seemed to be lost in deep thought. If he was thinking about what Jimmy figured he was, then trouble was brewing. The kid had to find a way to yank the trouble from inside the man's head.

"I wouldn't be concerned about that guy," Jimmy offered. "I think the storm caused him to panic a little. He's probably worried about getting home for Christmas. You know this weather might just keep a lot of folks from being with family this year."

"You could be right," Calvin wearily replied. "Unless it stops snowing, you're going to have trouble getting home tonight too."

"Yeah," Jimmy agreed, "and with our tree decorated and a candle in that holder you made, there are some special things to get home to."

The man's smile returned. "So you liked my gift?"

"It's perfect," came the quick reply. "Oh, I looked up that verse too."

"You mean Matthew 25:35-40?"

"Yeah," Jimmy said, "that's the one. It was underlined in Dad's Bible, so I guess he thought it was important too."

"Actually," Calvin confided, "he was the one who first shared it with me. Got me going to church too. I guess he was good at saving souls as well as lives."

"Could be," Jimmy replied.

It was a shame that his father couldn't save Jimmy tonight. But that wasn't possible. Likely the best he could hope for was not to be connected to the robbery. But with Calvin having seen Jake and him together, the bus driver might well figure things out. If he did, then everything would cave in on top of him.

"I've got something else to tell you about Dad, but not now. Maybe later at church." Jimmy assured the man as he pushed the door open and stepped out into the heavy snow.

Calvin nodded.

When Jimmy made it to the home's sweeping front porch, the car's wheels momentarily spun in the snow, then surged forward. The boy breathed a deep sigh of relief as the Ford headed south. Calvin wasn't going to the Thompson's house. Still, tomorrow morning, when word spread about the robbery, Jimmy figured odds were pretty good that the man who saved him today might convict him tomorrow. That thought was very sobering.

28

⚬⚬⚬

December 23, 1945, 5:20 p.m.

Jimmy spent ten minutes by himself in the room the Lankins called the parlor. Rarely used, the parlor was furnished with a dark-stained upright piano, three wingback chairs, a low coffee table, and a love seat. An area rug covered the hardwood floors. The room's defining feature, which made it so attractive, was its large, stone, corner fireplace. Yet as he paced the room, Jimmy didn't note any of this, nor did he study the dozen or so family photos framed and hanging on each side of the fireplace, the only thing on his mind was dealing with a world that was now completely out of control.

Initially, when Calvin had rescued him on the school grounds, Jimmy felt as if he'd escaped the trap. But as the clock ticked closer to when Jake would use that key to rob the store, the kid's insides were tangled up like fishing line. There were knots everywhere. Though he wasn't with Jake, he was still wearing those chains that Audrey had talked about in church. He was literally a slave to a choice, and there was no emancipator to free him. Where was the hope?

⚬⚬⚬

Jimmy glanced up at the clock on the mantel over the fire-place. It was five-twenty. He had less than an hour to come up with a plan. What could he do to make all the wrongs right?

His mind was spinning but getting nowhere when Audrey stomped the snow off her feet, opened the porch door, and walked into the room. She didn't bother pulling off her coat until she stood in front of the roaring fire. After she rubbed her hands together about a dozen times, she spoke, "I think I mentioned it was going to be a white Christmas."

Joining her in front of the fire, Jimmy suggested, "Maybe you should do weather on the radio." He waited for her expected giggle, then asked, "How was rehearsal?"

"It was good. I think this will be a very special service. I mean, so many families are together this year that haven't been together in years." The words had no more than escaped her lips than she turned toward Jimmy and said, "I'm sorry, I wasn't thinking."

He shook his head. "No, you're right, for so many people this is going to be an incredible holiday. Just because Dad's dead is no reason for me not to be happy for the others." He paused and grimly added, "In fact, Dad being dead is no excuse for anything."

"So you'll be at the service?" She turned her face back to the fire but touched his hand as she posed the question.

The answer should have been an easy one. He wanted to hear her sing more than anything in the world. He had planned on it, too, until just a few seconds ago. But now there was something else pulling him in another direction. The time for excuses and rationalizations for his actions was over. It was time for him to take charge of his life and rather than blame his father's death for his problems become like his father and take on those problems. The place to start was by righting a wrong, and being at church wasn't going to do that.

So while everyone else in town was listening to Audrey, he was going to be facing down his biggest fear. That meant he'd be taking on a man who had already shown he outmatched him in at least a dozen different ways. And Jake also had a gun. So if he couldn't beat Jimmy into submission, there was another option. But doing the right thing wasn't supposed to be easy, especially when that meant escaping a trap of his own construction.

"Jimmy."

He glanced from the fire to the girl. "Sorry, I was thinking about something else."

"I could tell. Was it that problem you were talking about yesterday?"

"Yeah," he admitted.

"I thought you had solved it. Isn't that what you told me last night?"

"Well," he replied soberly, "I had a plan then, but it was a shortcut and it wasn't really dealing with the mess I created. So now, thanks to you and dad and Calvin, I've got a new plan. One way or the other, that plan will get me right. And that is what I want. I want to do the right thing."

"I don't understand," she admitted, easing down to her knees in front of the fire.

Jimmy watched the light from the flames play across her face. She looked so much more mature than he figured he'd ever be. There was peace in her eyes, but more than that, there was a caring in her heart. It wasn't her father's money that made her rich, it was that caring heart.

He sat down beside her. As they both stared at the flames, he posed a question, "Who do you think is the richest man in town?"

Her reply was quick and somewhat defensive, "Well, it's not my dad, if that's what you're driving at."

"No," he softly assured her, "I don't mean that at all. What I'm talking about is a different kind of rich."

Her eyes turned to his. "I don't get you."

"It's funny, but the richest man I know is Calvin Jenkins."

She shook her head. "Your basic math skills aren't too sharp. You may need me to tutor you this next semester. If it wasn't for my father forgiving a few loans, Calvin would be out on the streets. He barely has a dime."

"I know," Jimmy replied, "but he has built a different kind of wealth. He stores his treasures in his heart and then shares them freely with everyone. In the last two days he taught me that it wasn't about what we have or what we have lost, it was about what we give."

"Your father was that way too," Audrey added. "I mean, think of those kids he was helping in the jungle and all the time he kept doing his job for the country. He could have played it safe, but he didn't."

"Yeah, he didn't play it safe. He just did what was right."

"Audrey, Jimmy," Mrs. Lankins called out from the back of the house, "you all need to get in here and eat something now or you won't get anything until after the service."

"Let's go grab some supper," Audrey suggested as she pushed herself off the floor.

"You go ahead," he said. "I've got something to do."

As he stood beside her, she grabbed his hand. Concern was etched deeply into her face and reflected in her voice as she whispered, "Are you sure about this?"

"Yeah," he said, smiling, "I'm sure. There is a wrong to be righted. I need to start being not just a Reed and standing for all that name has stood for, but I need to be like Calvin, too, and that means doing what a Christian should do."

As his explanation hung in the air, he felt like a new person. He'd never considered doing something because of faith until this moment, and that faith brought hope and that hope made him suddenly feel very grown-up.

As he was basking in a new sense of value, she surprised him. With no warning, Audrey pushed herself up on her tiptoes until her lips met his. She lingered there for a moment, then pulled back and whispered, "I don't know what this is all about, but whenever you finish you need to find me and tell me everything's OK."

He gently ran his fingers through her hair. "I will, and things will work out. Just have a little faith."

He grabbed his coat from off the chair, pulled it on, and stepped toward the door. As he felt the knob in his hand, he looked over his shoulder. "If you hear that I've done anything wrong or anyone says that I am a bad person, just remember, that guy was the Jimmy you knew before this moment. You keep that new Jimmy in your heart, and if anything happens, you hold onto that image of me. Don't ever forget I changed."

Pulling open the door, he walked out into the cold night. He was scared to death as he stepped off the porch and headed for downtown, but he was also no longer afraid of letting his mother or Audrey down. Yes, he might lose the battle he was about to wage, and he might well not even survive to see Christmas, but at least he would know he had lived long enough to become the man his father told Kevin Buck he was.

29

December 23, 1945, 6:10 p.m.

Jake checked his watch. He was already five minutes behind schedule, and it was all due to two unexpected factors. One was the heavy snow, and the other was the bus driver who happened upon him and the kid at the school. It was the latter that really messed things up. It forced him to play a card he didn't want to play. He'd have remained in town if it hadn't been for that. But if the bus driver had seen him hanging around Ash Flat, he might have called the sheriff. So though he didn't want to, good judgment demanded Jake drive the few miles outside of town to the stable and wait there. It was another lesson he'd learned in prison—being the center of attention was to be avoided at all costs. A smart crook never hung around when folks might be watching, and the old barn was the one place that offered certain solitude.

Still, while it was a safe refuge, the stable offered little physical or emotional comfort. For starters, it was cold and the six inches of fresh snow made it seem even colder. The weather had also turned the day into night. Thus, the old building was not only drafty but dark. Then there was the pile of straw in the corner of the room. That's where Frank had stashed Martin. Hence, there was the foreboding sense of death in the air and as the minutes dragged on, it spooked him. He knew it was not just stupid but also a sign of weakness. The normally composed Jake couldn't even look toward that corner of the stable for fear of seeing the very real Ghost of Christmas Present. So, when the pocket watch told him it was time to leave, he literally sprinted out the door and to the car.

Though the Hudson had difficulty driving back into the teeth of the storm, its relatively new tires had enough tread they did a pretty good job plowing through the frozen moisture. Because of the way the car clung to the road, he sensed his luck had changed. He knew that if there had been ice under the blanket of snow he would have never made it back into town. Yet he was in Ash Flat now, and no one was watching him as he arrived.

Rather than go directly to the store, Jake drove by the church. In spite of the horrid weather, the place looked packed. He pulled his car to a stop after he had driven a block past the old building, then killed the lights but left the Hudson idling, and trudged back to where everyone in town seemed to be riding out the storm. Standing beside the steps, he peered through the heavy flakes until he finally spotted the one car he was looking for. He now knew all he needed to know. The sheriff was at the service.

Turning on his heels, he hustled back to the Hudson, shifted into first and eased along the one block of buildings that comprised the community's business district. As Jake drove slowly past Miller's Store, he glanced through the passenger glass and into the store's front window; there were no lights or signs of life. The other stores were just as dead. Satisfied he had downtown to himself, he switched off his lights and made a right, drove to the back alley, and turned again. Pulling his car into an open space between two stores so that it would be hidden in case anyone drove by, he switched the motor off and slipped on the thin leather gloves he'd stolen for just this purpose. Grabbing his small bag of tools from the passenger side floorboard, he opened the door and stepped out into the unforgiving winter air.

Even though the storm was raging, he could still hear muffled music coming from the church. For all the wrong reasons this provided him with a great sense of peace. Secure in the knowledge that he had at last forty-five minutes to pull the job and get out of town, he made his way to the back door of Miller's Store. Setting the bag of tools in the snow, he reached into his right coat pocket and retrieved the key. Grinning, he squeezed it between his index finger and thumb and aimed it at the lock. It slipped right in.

After looking to his left and right to once more confirm he was alone, Jake twisted the key toward the right. It didn't move. He tried it again with the same result. Stepping back, he pulled it out and examined both the lock and the key. Satisfied they were in good condition, he again pushed the key back in. Once more, it failed to move.

Had the kid pulled one on him? Did he give him the wrong key? No, it went in too easily not to work. Maybe it was old enough it took some kind of special combination of turning while either lifting or pushing the doorknob. He didn't need to play that game when there was a second door that the key fit.

Picking up his bag, he hustled down the alley, made a left at the end of the alley, and slid around the corner and up to the front of the block. One quick peek proved he still had downtown to himself. Stepping up to the sidewalk, he rushed by Long's Grocery and Jim's Drug Store to Miller's. Once more dropping the bag in the snow, he pushed the key into the lock.

Once again it wouldn't turn. Falling to his knees, he jerked a flashlight out of the bag, turned it on, and aimed it at the lock.

"It's probably frozen."

Spinning to his feet, Jake looked for the person who owned the voice.

"How you doing, Jake?" Jimmy said as he stepped up onto the sidewalk.

"Your blasted key doesn't work," the man growled.

"No," Jimmy replied, "I've seen my mom use it a dozen times. I know it fits, but I think the weather has jimmied things up for you. The locks on our house get frozen up when we get this kind of snow and wind. I understand the back door at church froze up this afternoon. So, unless you have a blow torch in the bag, you aren't going to get the key to open the door tonight."

As Jake glared at him, Jimmy chuckled and added, "I think I got my miracle."

The weather was the one thing Jake hadn't planned for. Yet a frozen lock was no miracle, and it was not going to stop him now. He still had plenty of time to pull the job and get out of town. Setting the flashlight back into the bag, he retrieved a hammer.

"That's going to make a lot of noise," Jimmy hollered over the strong north wind.

"Yeah," Jake laughed, "but with all the music going on down the street, no one will hear it."

As the muffled strains of "Joy to the World" filtered through the heavy snow and wind, the man turned, pulled back his arm and aimed for the showroom window. Before he ever got the chance to swing, Jimmy went into action. With the snow muffling his steps, the kid grabbed the larger man from behind. The slippery sidewalk made dragging the thief to the ground an easy task. Yet once the much stronger Jake turned and got his left hand on Jimmy, the tide quickly turned and the fight was literally over before it began.

"You just made your last stupid move," Jake hissed as he brought a fist to Jimmy's gut. Jimmy's coat took away a bit of the power, but the blow still forced all the air from his lungs. As he struggled for breath, Jake gained the clear advantage. Rolling on top of the boy, he pinned Jimmy's arm to the ground with his knees.

"Any last words, kid?"

Still trying to regain his breath, Jimmy set his jaw and shook his head.

"You said something about a miracle," Jake snorted. "Well, I don't see one coming."

A sick grin on his lips, the enraged man lifted the hammer and carefully aimed it at the boy's head. As he did, Jimmy closed his eyes and waited for a crushing blow that never came.

30

December 23, 1945, 6:25 p.m.

"Jake, let the boy go."

The voice was familiar, but not so familiar that it immediately drew an image in Jimmy's head. He knew he'd heard it before, but where?

Opening his eyes, Jimmy saw Jake with the raised ball-peen hammer still hovering over his head. Yet Jimmy was no longer the focus of Jake's attention. His eyes were fixed on a place out in the street.

"No!" Jake screamed as he lowered his arm and jumped up.

Suddenly free, Jimmy rolled over onto his stomach and pushed himself upright. He took three quick steps down the walk before turning to try to see who had saved his life. Squinting in a fruitless attempt to peer through the heavy snow, he could only make out the outline of a thin man standing just a few feet from the sidewalk steps. The snow was simply too heavy and the night too dark to identify him. But "the who" was not nearly as important as "the what" and "the what" was that he had been saved from the executioner's swing. Like his father on that day when he faced the Japanese in the Philippines, Jimmy had a second chance at life. Now, he had to make the most of it.

Glancing back toward Jake, he noted the man had tossed the hammer to the ground and pulled out the flashlight. He flipped it on and aimed the beam at the third man. The lights reflected off the falling snow and made the figure on the street glow.

"You can't be here," Jake cried out, his voice trembling. "You're dead. I saw Frank kill you this morning. I saw him drag your body into the stable."

"Funny that you should call that old barn a stable. It was in a stable a long time ago that a miracle happened that started this holiday."

"What?" Jake roared. "You expect me to believe you were somehow brought back to life?"

"I don't care what you believe, but if you think I'm dead, then I must be a ghost. So you can just call me the Ghost of Christmas Present. And you will be a ghost, too, if you hurt the kid. I came back to this world to stop you."

Maybe it was because he couldn't fathom what it all meant, but Jake couldn't take his eyes off the scene playing out in front of him. So Jimmy had a chance to flee down the street and escape the monster that just moments ago could and would have easily smashed his skull. But just like Jake, the kid could not move either.

"Jake," the visitor shouted over the wind, "you remember that dream I had?"

Jake nodded and licked his lips.

"Well, that's all a part of this. See, I didn't understand it then, but now I know that home wasn't Mississippi. That's where I was wrong. Home is a lot farther away than the old farm my folks live on. But there's something I got to do first. You see, I have to make things right before I get to go home."

It was obvious Jake wasn't following what Martin was saying. So, while Jimmy was curious as to where home was and what the man had to do to get there, Jake was much more interested in something else.

"How did you get here?" he barked.

The answer was much simpler than Jake probably expected. "Hitched a ride with you, Jake. You see, I'm a walking, talking dead man. Guess they never told you about that when you got your prison education. I was heading down the lane at the stable toward town, in fact toward this very spot, when I saw you drive up. As you killed time in the stable, I crawled into the backseat, slipped to the floorboard, and waited."

The flashlight was now shaking in Jake's hand. Though he was obviously confused and scared, he wasn't ready to give up taking the money from Miller's Store. No matter that a man claiming to be dead was talking to him, the crook still tried to stay in touch with his master plan.

"If you want your money," Jake shouted, "I'll give you half of your haul. But you'll have to get the rest out of Frank. We split it. And you can have half of what I get out of the safe in the store too. It's all yours. After all, we're partners."

The man in the street shrugged and raised his palms. As he did, Jake grew even more agitated.

"Listen, Martin," Jake pleaded, "I didn't charge you and I didn't hit you. I didn't even try to stop you from leaving. That was Frank. You shouldn't have any bone to pick with me. I was always fair to you. So I still want you to get your share of this job."

"Awfully nice of you," Martin shot back, "but what good is money to a ghost?"

Keeping the light trained on his former partner, Jake reached into his pocket and pulled out his pistol. With ten feet of ground and three steps separating the two of them, it was clear who should have had the advantage. But the hand holding the gun was now shaking so hard Jimmy doubted Jake could hit much of anything.

"You can't kill me," Martin boasted, "I'm already dead. Remember, you watched Frank bury me under that straw. Go ahead, aim at my heart and empty your gun. It might stagger me, but it won't stop me. You can't stop a ghost! Come on, Jake, fill my heart with lead and find out I'm immune to lead poisoning."

As a fascinated Jimmy looked on, Martin slowly moved forward. He took two steps in the snow and stopped. As he looked down at the unwelcome visitor, Jake froze, uncertain as to what to do next. So it was Martin's move, and the thin man stepped onto the first step of the store. As Martin planted his right foot, Jake pulled the trigger. The gun fired, shooting a flame out into night. The bullet rang like a bell when it hit his body, but it didn't cause Martin to hesitate, much less stop. Two steps, three chimes, and four shots later, Martin still moved steadily toward his former comrade. Jake pulled his trigger for a final time and, again, the bullet had no effect.

When Martin got to Jake, he grabbed him by the collar with both hands and pushed him backward. The power of that shove, combined with the slippery sidewalk, propelled the man into and through the glass showcase window. Martin followed him into the store, delivering two lefts and two rights to Jake's jaw. Those four blows knocked the man out, and he lay limp beside a barrel that was being used to display Christmas wrapping paper. Martin stared at his former boss for a few moments before stepping from the window. Once he was on the sidewalk, he swept glass from his jacket as he moved slowly to the door. Reaching out, he removed the key, studied it momentarily, then tossed it to the boy. After Jimmy caught it, the man smiled.

"Kid, that key is the only thing that connects you to this. With his record, anything Jake says that drags you into this will be viewed as a lie. You can walk away now and no one will ever be wiser. And I recommend you never visit the wrong side of the street again."

A still-confused Jimmy pondered the words for a few seconds. Looking toward the store window and back at the figure who'd saved his life, he posed a question: "How come bullets can't stop you?"

Martin grinned, unbuttoned his coat, reached inside, and pulled out a huge grain shovel blade, "That's why I dared him to shoot at my heart. If he'd aimed at my head, I'd have been in trouble."

Shoving the dented piece of rusty metal under his arm, Martin looked back at the man now decorating the showroom window. He studied him for a moment, then noted something on the sidewalk. He bent over and picked up Jake's pocket watch. He tossed it back into the snow and laughed, "Jake, it seems you're out of time."

Turning back to the kid, he made a request, "I need to ask you a favor."

"Sure," Jimmy answered.

"I think remaining dead might be the best way for me to start a new life. So give me a couple of minutes to disappear before you go get the sheriff. And then you take credit for capturing Jake."

"But," Jimmy argued, "he'll tell them about you."

Martin laughed, "He'll tell them about a ghost that couldn't be stopped. Do you really think anyone is going to believe that? Besides, you stood up to him. So you were a part of stopping him as well. You keeping him busy set him up for me to take him down."

Martin stepped down from the steps and onto the street. As he disappeared into the storm, he hollered, "Merry Christmas, kid."

Within a minute of Martin leaving, the wind died and the heavy snow quit and Jimmy could clearly hear the music coming from the church. Once more, it was Audrey singing "O Holy Night." The boy smiled; he might not have been the one who actually stopped Jake, but by taking a step on faith and standing up to him, he was no longer a slave to his own actions or to the bitterness caused by his father's death. In fact, he understood why his dad had done what he'd done. For the first time, that medal his mother so treasured now meant something to him as well.

31

December 23, 1945, 8:15 p.m.

A calm and thankful Jimmy was now sitting in the back room at the Methodist church munching on homemade Christmas cookies. Across the long folding table, Audrey, her shoulder-length honey-colored hair catching the overhead light, was puzzled. She couldn't begin to fathom how the skinny boy had stopped a robbery, and she couldn't understand why Jimmy wasn't sharing any details with her.

"How did you know?" she asked again. "I mean, you were there right when it happened."

"I told you," he smiled, "I had the key."

"Actually," Calvin said as he drew up a chair beside the boy, "I had it, too, and didn't act on it."

"What do you two mean?" Audrey demanded. "I'm not following any of this."

"Well," the bus driver began, "this guy tracked Jimmy down today to supposedly ask directions. I was suspicious at that moment, but I had a few gifts to deliver so I quickly forgot about him. Thankfully, Jimmy didn't and went back downtown to make sure everything was all right. That's when he found the guy breaking into the store. I feel guilty for not being there to help."

"But how did you have the courage to face him?" Audrey demanded, turning her now adoring gaze back to the teen.

Jimmy shrugged. He couldn't tell the whole story. If he did, he'd have to go back on his word to the man who'd really stopped Jake. But he wasn't going to lie either. So, rather than say anything, he just left it the way it was. Jake was off the streets and in jail, his mother was safe, and he had learned a great deal about taking shortcuts in life. If he was lucky, that would be the end of it.

A cold draft swept into the room as the back door opened. Walking in from the bitter cold was Sheriff Phil Thompson. Following behind were Clark Miller and Mark Dietz.

"You men need some coffee?"

They each nodded toward Audrey's mom as they removed their coats. A few moments later, cups of steaming liquid in their hands, they joined Jimmy, Audrey, and Calvin at the table. It was the bus driver who popped the first question.

"So, did you all figure out who he is?"

After taking a sip of black coffee, Thompson nodded. "He's a small-time crook who once spent a couple of years in prison. His name is Jake Simpson. We already know he was responsible for the robbery in Salem earlier this month because he had the marked bills from that job on him. He's also wanted for a series of robberies last summer in Missouri. I have a feeling that we'll find he has been a part of a dozen or more before the investigation concludes."

Savoring another taste of the hot brew, the sheriff continued, "The guy seems a bit daft. He claims he had a partner who killed a man named Martin Crane this morning. They hid his body under some straw in an old barn on the Anderson place. I had Mark drive out there and take a look and that is where the guy's story begins to develop more holes than a moth-eaten wool suit."

Dietz nodded. "I searched that old barn over from top to bottom. It was pretty obvious someone had been holed up there for a few days, but there was no body anywhere."

"Strange," Calvin chimed in. "Why would a guy claim to be a part of a murder and tell us where to find the body when there was no body?"

"That confused me too," Thompson agreed, "but what he told me next made even less sense. He claimed the man his partner killed, this guy named Crane, was the one who pushed him through the window and knocked him out. He kept calling him the Christmas ghost and said he couldn't be killed."

"Either the guy really is crazy," Miller added, "or he is setting himself up for some kind of very unique defense when all of this plays out in court."

"Well," Dietz said, "I know Crane is a real guy. He came into my store and bought a candy bar. He also registered for the toy tractor I'm giving away."

"And he was probably involved with Simpson," the sheriff broke in, "because he paid Mark with a bill taken during the robbery at Salem. But he's sure not dead and in the barn, and Mark saw him clearly enough to know he's no ghost either. And there were some extra footprints in the snow—doubt those were made by a ghost."

While those gathered at the table and those standing off to one side listening considered the strange confession, Jimmy grimly smiled. These ramblings of a supposed lunatic were much closer to the truth than the sheriff would ever know. Jake wasn't crazy, he was simply scared to death and he had every right to be. After all, he'd emptied his gun into a shiny figure in the snow and it had done nothing. That would leave anyone overwhelmed. Jimmy had been there to watch it and still couldn't fully believe it wasn't some kind of miracle, starting with the frozen locks and ending with Jake going into the window.

"Anything else?" Audrey asked.

"Yeah," Thompson turned to look at Jimmy as he explained, "It seems Jimmy has a part in this too."

The boy's heart literally stopped. As a dozen sets of eyes shifted his way, Jimmy squirmed in his chair. Yet this time he didn't want to run. He was ready to 'fess up. He was just clearing his throat to admit what he'd done when the sheriff continued his take on the story. His words only made the boy feel guiltier.

"I would have never thought Jimmy Reed would have been capable of something like this."

It was obvious the sheriff had figured it out. The fact he'd secretly dropped the key back into his mother's purse fifteen minutes before made no difference now. Jake had squealed and Thompson knew at least one part of his crazy tale was true.

The sheriff took another sip of coffee, shook his head, and continued, "Jimmy, I wish you'd brought this to me."

The boy nodded. It was time to get everything off his chest. "I should have told you from the beginning."

"Yeah," the law officer agreed, "you took a terrible risk."

Marge, who'd been standing off to the side with Kevin Buck, approached the table. She was confused. Like most of the others in the room, she couldn't understand the direction the story had taken.

"Phil," she softly asked, "are you trying to say James was somehow involved with this Simpson guy?"

"Yeah, your son was playing a very dangerous game. The part about Jimmy is the one segment of the guy's story that makes perfect sense, and the more I mull it over the more upset I get. What your son did was just plain stupid."

Jimmy smiled bleakly. It was time to level with them and embrace the truth. It wasn't going to be easy, because the pain was going to go far beyond his own. He hated to break his mother's heart, but at least he'd tried to fix things at the end. When she found that out, it would help, and he was sure that in time she'd forgive him. He looked over at Audrey, and he could tell by her expression she still had faith in him. And before he'd left her house this evening, he'd given her a cryptic message that she'd be able to figure out now. Surely, because he was a part of catching Jake, the courts would go a bit easier on him. At least that was the hope.

After downing another sip of coffee, Thompson looked over at Jimmy and continued, "There were originally two more guys in the gang. One was this Crane, who Simpson claimed is dead, and the other was a man named Frank Pelton. It seems Jimmy met both of these men."

"That's right, sir," Jimmy answered, his voice strong and clear. "I met them in the Anderson stable."

Thompson looked back at the teen. "And you knew from the get-go they were up to no good."

"Yes, sir," Jimmy replied.

"James," Marge whispered, "you knew these men?"

"He did," Thompson answered for the boy. "He knew their plans to rob Clark's place. And as soon as he had the information, he should have brought it to me. But the more I ponder on this, the more I'm convinced he didn't come to me because of his father's winning the Medal of Honor. Isn't that right?"

"Yes, sir," Jimmy acknowledged. "I've always had some mixed-up feelings about that. It was kind of hard to live up to the standards of a man like Dad."

"I'm sure it is," the sheriff agreed. Thompson studied Jimmy for a few seconds and then turned back to the small crowd now hanging on his every word.

"According to Simpson, Jimmy outsmarted him. The boy literally set him up. He played along with the plan only so that he could catch the men in the act. It was a move that was as stupid as it was brave. It is the stupid part that might have gotten him killed and makes me a little angry with him."

"I don't understand," Marge said. "What do you mean James set him up?"

"Jimmy," the sheriff declared, "was able to catch the guy in the act because he knew when it was coming down. Jimmy, I still don't fully understand how you overpowered the guy."

"I didn't," Jimmy argued.

"Well," Thompson said, "maybe the slick sidewalk helped, but it was obvious you two struggled pretty good before Simpson ended up out like a light in the showroom window. Anyway, according to Simpson that's the story."

Clark Miller chimed in, "Not all the story. Remember what he said was his big mistake?"

"What was that?" Marge asked.

Miller smiled, "He told us he went wrong when he put his hopes in an honest boy."

Marge came over and placed her hands on her son's shoulders. Pride was evident in her face. "Phil, are the roads clear enough for someone to take us home?"

"Yeah," Calvin jumped in, "I can take you. I need to be heading home anyway."

"It'll take me a few minutes to help clean up this room and get my things," Marge said apologetically.

"That'll be fine," Calvin answered. "It will give me time to go out and get the old Ford warmed up. Just come out when you're ready."

As Audrey and the others jumped up to clear the table, Jimmy pushed his chair back, grabbed his coat, and followed Calvin out to the car. After the bus driver started the old V-8 and they were both seated in the sedan's front seat, Jimmy broke the silence.

"It really wasn't the way the sheriff said it was."

"You don't say," Calvin replied.

"There was nothing noble about what I did until the very end."

The older man nodded. "Sometimes you have to walk in the darkness for a while to really appreciate the light."

"But Calvin . . ."

"No more," the man's unexpectedly sharp tone stopped the boy in midsentence. "Jimmy, you might have gotten involved in something for the wrong reasons, but somewhere along the way you figured that out and you found a way to correct the mistake in judgment you made. Second chances are about as good a Christmas gift as any of us can get."

"But they don't know the whole truth," the boy argued.

"They know the truth that matters," Calvin assured him.

"What's that?"

"Jimmy, they see the way your heart is now. They will find hope because you've changed."

"So, Calvin, you think God did this just to teach me a lesson?"

"I'm a farmer who drives a bus; I don't have answers for big questions like that. Maybe this was set in motion so that Jake could get caught before he actually killed someone. Maybe you being a part of it had to happen to save the life of a person we will never meet. Or maybe you were there to help a few merchants in other towns get their money back. Or maybe it was your presence that helped that Crane guy change the direction in his life. As you can see, the maybes could go on forever."

"Calvin, you make it sound like it was all part of a plan."

"Could be," he said, "but might not be too. The important thing at this moment is you changed."

Jimmy nodded. "Calvin, you were a part of that change. Your words, your example of visiting the people you visit and the way you help them. Your stories about my dad and the way he lived. Even that candleholder and the light it brought made an impact on me. And then there was that Bible verse. It made me open my dad's Bible and get to know him in a way I'd never known him before."

Jimmy's jaw dropped. "The envelope! I'd forgotten all about it."

"What envelope?" Calvin asked.

"The one I found in Dad's Bible that I was supposed to open three Christmases ago. I have to open it now. We have to get home right now so I can see what's in it."

"Let's at least wait for your mother."

Jimmy, who just a few minutes before had felt so grown up, was once again a kid. There was a Christmas present waiting, one that had been waiting a long time, and he couldn't and wouldn't wait for the twenty-fifth to open it. It had to be done tonight!

32

December 23, 1945, 10:45 p.m.

Jimmy had charged into his home and ripped into the envelope as soon they had gotten home. He was both shocked and disappointed that the only contents were a simple handwritten letter.

Dear Son,

This will be your first Christmas without me. I wish I could be there with you, but I have something to do that is far bigger than my wishes. One of the things that I will miss the most are our holiday traditions. Remember this, wherever I am I will be picturing us cutting down a tree, stringing popcorn, and singing carols. I will also be watching you move the nativity scene pieces around as the Christmas story is read. Knowing that those things will continue is why I placed this letter where you could easily find it on Christmas Eve.

So now that I can picture you reading the letter and wondering what it is all about, let me cut to the chase. There are three presents I have hidden around the farm that are just for this year. Each is special to me, and I hope each will come to mean something to you as well. And I am not going to make this easy; I'm going to make you work for them. The clues I am writing will lead you to the gifts if you are smart enough to figure them out.

1. One of the wise men brought this as a gift for the baby Jesus. Knowing where that present was delivered and how those visitors from the east found the location will lead you to your first gift.

2. I've likely never told you about my hero. He isn't an athlete or an entertainer. He is a man who has devoted his life to service to others. He once gave a speech that summed up what I think is the key to happiness. You will find this gift by remembering where a key is stored that doesn't unlock any doors, but still has the power to make work easier.

3. The final gift is one that will speak only if you have the machine to translate its message. A clue to lead you to this special gift is for you to consider the shape of the instrument that Gabriel blows.

Merry Christmas, Jimmy, and I hope your Christmas wishes for this year come true, and I promise I will be home when all of this is over to once again share our traditions with you and Mom. I am clinging to that hope!

Love, Dad

Jimmy leaned back against his headboard. This was not what he expected, and so as he pondered the clues a wave of disappointment rushed over him. As the note clearly said, these gifts were hidden around the farm, but he couldn't get involved in the treasure hunt tonight. That meant he'd have to wait until there was light. It looked like his Christmas, which was already three years overdue, was going to have to wait for one more day.

33

December 24, 1945, 9:17 a.m.

J immy had just finished his morning chores and was in his bedroom reading his father's letter once again when he heard the sounds of a car struggling down their snow-covered lane. Drawing back the curtain, he noted the Millers' long, dark Buick. Behind the wheel was his mother's boss.

Grabbing his coat, the boy shoved the letter into his pocket and stepped out onto the porch. He waited there until Clark Miller stepped out of the vehicle.

"Jimmy, merry Christmas!"

Jimmy's smile matched the storeowner's. Jumping off the porch, he jogged across the yard, the snow crunching under his feet. "Merry Christmas to you, sir."

After shaking the boy's hand, Miller studied him as if sizing up the boy for a suit, then brought his gloved fingers together, looked directly into the boy's eyes, and announced, "Jimmy, I came out here for two reasons. The first was to thank you for what you did last night. I agree with Sheriff Thompson that you shouldn't have tried to do this on your own, but I am proud of you nevertheless. If your father were here, I know he'd be proud of you too."

Fighting a sense of guilt, Jimmy shrugged. "You're making too big a deal out of this. It was the ghost who did the hard work, don't you remember? I mean, you heard it from the crook's mouth."

"Yeah," Miller laughed, "but ghost or not, you still deserve a reward. I want to give you twenty-five dollars."

The man reached into his coat pocket and pulled out two tens and a five. Jimmy studied them for a moment, but made no move to take them.

"Come on, son, this is for you. You deserve it."

"No, sir," the kid modestly replied, "I really don't. And I don't want them either."

Miller looked hurt. "Jimmy, I really want you to have this money. I want you to buy something you need, and I'm not going to take no for an answer."

"Mr. Miller, my dad didn't take things when he did something for others and I'm not going to either. In fact, if Dad were here, he probably would have argued that others were much more qualified for the Medal of Honor than he was. You have to understand, my goal is to be like he was. So you just keep your money. Your thanks is much more of a reward than I deserve. The good Lord knows that. I mean, He really does!"

The storeowner's shocked expression proved he was not expecting this response. He glanced down at the cash in his hand before shaking his head and spitting out something he likely deemed was pure logic, "You could buy a lot with this much money. If you don't want to get something for yourself, you could get something for someone else. Besides, if you don't take this twenty-five dollars, I'm just going to give it to someone else anyway. So why don't you take the decision of what to do with it off my shoulders?"

A picture suddenly flashed in Jimmy's head. As it grew sharper, he grinned and glanced up at Miller. "Last night, my mom told me you gave her a bonus."

"I did," Miller proudly announced, "and it really wasn't as big as it should have been. She's the best worker I've ever had."

"Then could you kind of give her the reward you're trying to give me? She deserves it more than I do."

Miller nodded. "I guess I could do that."

"But, Mr. Miller, don't give her the cash, 'cause she'd likely just buy something for me and that's not what I want this Christmas. There's a French perfume she really loves that you have in a display case. I can't even begin to say the name, but it costs twenty-five dollars."

"You mean L'Heure Bleue?"

"Yeah, that sounds like it."

"I could do that, Jimmy, but my cost is less than the twenty-five, so there would be some money left over."

"OK," Jimmy smiled, "use what's left to buy a Perry Como record for Audrey. She's been a peach over the last few days, and she deserves a real Christmas surprise too."

"Sure, what record?"

"Till the End of Time."

"Good choice," Miller assured him, "but there will still be a few dollars left."

"Then give it to someone in town you consider—what's that term in the Bible—oh, yeah, the least of these."

"I can do that, Jimmy. I know of a family that likely can't buy presents for their three kids."

"Then you have everything taken care of," Jimmy explained. "And this works out just super for everyone too!"

Miller pushed the money back into his pocket. "You're full of surprises."

"You don't know the half," Jimmy answered. "You said you had two reasons for coming out here this morning? I think we have taken care of the first one. What was the other? Is there something you need?"

"Yeah, since the end of the war, business has really picked up. We are carrying more merchandise than ever before. I was hoping you might consider taking a job at the store. It would just be after school on weekdays and Saturday, but I could really use you."

"Yeah," Jimmy said, "that would be nice."

"So you will take it?"

"Yes, sir. And I'll work hard, and you can trust me too." Jimmy really emphasized the last part.

"Great. Come on in the first day after school starts. Now I need to get back to the store; we're really going to be busy today, and I left your mother and Clara there to handle it. I need to be there to help them. And I'll get those gifts wrapped and make sure they get back to you so you can give them to the folks you mentioned."

"Thanks for everything, sir."

Jimmy stood in the snow-covered yard as Miller got back into his car and turned around. The boy watched the Buick slip along the lane until it reached the highway. He was just about to begin his treasure quest when another unexpected guest turned into the lane. He knew the car and the driver well, so he held his spot until Audrey shut off her motor and stepped out into the crisp air.

"Hey," he said, grinning.

"Hey, yourself," she laughed. "And don't make fun of the way I'm dressed. Dad made me wear jeans today because he was afraid I'd slide into a ditch coming out here and he didn't want me to wade through the snow in a dress."

"You look great, and you're dressed perfectly to help me find three special gifts."

She smiled as she trudged up to him. "I don't understand. In fact, I've still pretty confused about last night."

"So am I," he grinned. "But come inside and I'll explain today's mystery to you. And then maybe you can help me get to know my dad a bit better."

"I'm still confused," she laughed, "but could we do something before we go in?"

Jimmy glanced up at the hardwood tree he was standing under. Mr. Collins had explained all about mistletoe and now it was time to put that knowledge into action. "Audrey, look up above us."

She glanced up into the tree. "Jimmy, I don't know what this is all about but . . ." His lips met hers and she never finished her thought.

"Wow," she sighed a few seconds later.

"Was that what you wanted?" he asked.

She smiled. "Actually no. I just wanted to give you the gift I got for you."

Jimmy blushed. "So you didn't know we were standing under mistletoe?"

"No," she admitted, "and by the way, I only kiss boys I really, really like."

"Oh." The boy fumbled for something to say and came up empty.

"And I really, really like you, Jimmy."

He took a deep breath, the smile returning to his face.

"This is for you," she said as she held something out to him. "Sorry it's not wrapped. I didn't know if you had your own Bible. And even if you do, I doubt you have one with your name on the front."

Taking it, he ran his finger over the gold letters that spelled out "James Reed" and smiled. "We are about to put this to use."

"What do you mean?" she asked.

"Come on in and you'll find out."

34

December 24, 1945, 11:13 a.m.

They walked in circles around the barn, as Audrey read the first clue for the tenth time. "I just don't get it. I mean the gift has to be either spices or money. I would guess the latter is much more likely. But what does the location have to do with it?"

"I don't know," Jimmy admitted. "I mean, we have looked all over the barn and that's the closest thing we have to a stable. We even checked the hay loft and searched for any loose boards."

"And I looked between the logs in the outside walls too," she added. She sat down on an upside-down milk bucket and shook her head. "You sure have a lot of stuff stored out here."

"A lot of junk, you mean," he laughed. "Did you see that mess in the loft?"

"Yeah. I kind of liked that old table. It could be refinished and would look really good beside a bed."

"Sure," he sarcastically observed, "if you actually could find the missing leg."

ACE COLLINS

"Well, there is that," she admitted. "But the wind-up record player looked like it might still work."

"Could be," he replied, "but none of the stuff you're pointing out gets us any closer to answering the first mystery, and I don't want to go to the second one until we get this first one licked."

As if she'd sat on a tack, Audrey bolted up right and grinned. "And that's because we've been looking in the wrong place."

"What?" he asked. "What else do we have that is even close to a stable?"

"Nothing," she smugly explained, "but the wise men didn't go to the stable. Only the shepherds saw Jesus there. Think back to what we just read in that Bible I gave you."

Jimmy was confused. "I'm drawing a blank. I thought they came along about the same time as the shepherds."

Audrey shook her head, "You weren't listening when I read, were you?"

"I was kind of, but I was also pushing the figures around the nativity scene. When you got to the part about the visitors from the east, I pushed them over to the manger."

"Jimmy, that's not where they went to see the baby Jesus."

"Really? Then where was it?"

"In the home where Mary and Joseph lived," Audrey said as she moved out of the barn and marched toward the house. She was already on the porch before Jimmy caught up with her. He was right behind her as they entered the living room.

"Do you have any stars in your house?"

Jimmy tilted his head to the right and considered her query. As he did, Audrey made a sweep of the living room before heading to the kitchen. "I don't see any in here," she cried out.

"I know of one," Jimmy almost yelled. Falling to his knees, he quickly inventoried the twenty or so books in the bookcase. "Look at the stuff on top of the case."

"OK," she said. Pointing to a glass vase with a star etching on the right side, she laughed, "It was right in front of our noses, so why are you looking below the star?"

"Didn't you read they followed the star to the house?" Jimmy said.

"Yes, they did," she acknowledged.

"And you thought I wasn't listening," he teased. "Anyway, it has to be in the books or be one of the books. The problem is there are no books under the vase that are about homes. And I just leafed through the Bible and there's nothing hidden in there either."

"Under the star," she whispered as her fingers went below the shelf the vase sat on. Smiling, she said, "Here it is," and leaned over to look. "There's an envelope taped to the bottom of this board."

Jimmy pushed his hand over the books and to the area hidden by a decorative piece of trim. She was right—there was something there. Finding a corner, he pulled the envelope free and brought it out. Audrey leaned over his shoulder as the boy quickly tore into the white envelope. As soon as he had it open, a coin dropped to the floor.

"It's gold, Jimmy," she whispered. "It's an old coin."

"There's a note with it. Let me read it."

As Audrey picked up the gold piece, Jimmy read the note out loud. "Your name is the gold standard. How you carry that name will determine what people think of you. And more than that, how you live your life, the decisions you make, reflect on the name of Christ. As a Christian, you carry his name as well. Other people will see faith and hope in your actions. This twenty-dollar gold piece was your great-grandfather's. He gave it to his son, who gave it to me. Now it is yours. Don't spend it; instead keep it with you to remind you to live to the highest standards."

"Wow," Audrey said, "this is like a family heirloom."

"How different my life would have been," Jimmy sighed, "if I had found this gift in 1942."

"I don't understand," she said. "Do you mean the way you've gotten into a bit of trouble at school?"

"Yeah," he laughed, "and a few other things too. But that is behind me."

Taking the 1849 Liberty coin from the girl, he studied it for only a second and then slipped it into his pocket. "Well, we have two more to find. What did the next clue say?"

"It was about your dad's personal hero and a key that didn't unlock doors."

Jimmy nodded and smiled. He'd seen a key that didn't unlock a door last night, but that was something much different than what his father was hinting at. So where on the farm was a key that didn't unlock a door?

"Any ideas?" she asked.

"I've got one," he assured her. "There's a key on the wall in the chicken coop. I've never known what it fit. In fact, I've never really studied it, just kind of noticed it and left it there. But logic tells me it would have to be for something in that building. Let's go take a look."

The key was hanging on a hook just inside the door. It was a skeleton-type key, rusty and small. As Jimmy picked it up, Audrey explored the small six-by-eight-foot shed.

"I don't see anything that even takes a lock."

"I've been in here hundreds of times," he mumbled, "and I don't remember anything either."

Patting it against his palm, he tried to think of something other than a door that had a slot for a key. "Wasn't there a small box in the barn that had a lock on it?"

"Yes," Audrey replied, "it was black. I remember picking it up and . . ."

He didn't let her finish before bolting from the chicken coop and racing back toward the log barn. He charged in and quickly stepped over to an area his father had used as a workbench. There, between two fruit jars filled with nails, was the box. It was no more than eight inches wide, four inches high, and four inches deep. It appeared to be homemade. Jimmy slipped the key into the lock and gave it a twist. It opened right up.

"Got it," he laughed. Yet lifting the lid wiped away his smile. The inside of the box was completely empty.

Audrey shrugged. "Must not be the key we're looking for."

"Guess not," Jimmy sighed, still peering into the box as if he expected something to magically appear. "But I just don't know of any other keys."

Sitting down on a bale of hay, he reached over to the bench and picked up an old brace and bit that was sitting on a lower wooden shelf. Lost in thought, he twisted the ancient mechanical drill in his hands and inventoried everything on the farm that might take a key. Logic told him it would have to be something they never used or they would have already discovered the present. So what could it be, and where was it?

After stretching, the girl moved over to the selection of tools and played with a large screwdriver, using it to twist a loose screw further into the wall. She then moved over to pick up a drill bit. "Does this go in that thing you've got?"

He looked up and nodded, "Yeah, it could. You just slide in the bottom and tighten it up by turning . . ."

He grinned. "That must be it. Right before Dad left, he won a drill in a contest at the hardware store. It was one of those power jobs. He thought it was funny because we didn't have electricity in the barn so it wasn't going to be much good for him. He talked about running a wire out here, but never did."

"What does that have to do with anything?" she asked.

"With electric drills you tighten the bits with a key," he explained. "Now, where is that box? You see, because we didn't use it much, he kept it in the box it came in."

Jimmy set the brace and bit down and looked around the workbench. There was no sign of it. As the barn was never locked and it didn't have electricity, he doubted his father would have stored it out here. But where was it? Of course, it was under the kitchen sink!

"Come on," he barked, grabbing Audrey's hand and leading her back into the snow.

"You know where it is?" she panted as they entered the house again.

He didn't answer as he sprinted back to the kitchen and opened the cabinet doors. There was the box. He pulled it out and hurriedly placed it on the table. Reaching in, he yanked out the drill and then a couple of bits. "Eureka!" he laughed as he found the chuck key. Setting it to one side, he peered into the almost empty box. There was another envelope and something in a small wooden frame. He grabbed the envelope first and tore into it.

"What's it say?" Audrey demanded.

"Jimmy, my hero is the missionary doctor Albert Schweitzer. In the frame are words to live by. It was a quote he gave to some students who were searching for ways to find fulfillment in their lives. Like Schweitzer, I think the spice of life is not money or fame, but it can be found by helping others. Life is so much sweeter when you aren't wrapped up in selfishness. So please hang this on your wall and think about it once a day."

Jimmy's hand shot back into the box and pulled out the framed document. The quote was not long, and the message was simple but profound.

I don't know what your destiny will be, but I do know that the only ones among you who will truly be happy are those who have sought and found how to serve.

"I guess my dad was the happiest man on the planet," Jimmy said. "From what Calvin and Mr. Buck and a bunch of others have said, he really knew what it was to serve others."

"Gold and a spice," Audrey smiled.

"What do you mean?" Jimmy said as their eyes met.

"The gifts, the wise men brought gold and spices to Jesus. That is what frankincense and myrrh are. They were rare spices. So you have a gold coin that reminds you of charac-ter and a framed quote that shows how to season your life so you are happy. It seems to me your dad was a pretty wise man too."

"Yeah," Jimmy nodded. "I'm starting to figure that out too."

"One more to go," Audrey noted. As Jimmy restudied the words in the frame, she picked up the letter and read the instructions for the last gift. "The final gift is one that will speak only if you have the machine to translate its message. A clue to lead you to this special gift is to consider the shape of the instrument that Gabriel blows."

"It was a trumpet, wasn't it?" Jimmy asked.

"You have any ram horns around?" Audrey joked.

"No," he replied, "we don't have any horns of any kind."

"So let's think about something that translates," she sug-gested. "Do you have any foreign language dictionaries?"

"No," he assured her, "and a book wouldn't be a machine that translates anyway. It has to be something mechanical."

She snapped her fingers. "I know. It's in the barn. We saw it earlier in the loft. I am absolutely sure of it. Come on."

Placing the framed quote back on the table, the two hurried past the Christmas tree, out of the house, and into the yard. This time Audrey was leading the way. She charged through the door and up the ladder to the hayloft. By the time Jimmy had joined her, she was in the corner, her hands tracing the horn on an old wind-up Victrola.

"A record player translates grooves into music," she explained.

Jimmy sat down beside her and opened the hinged top. There was a final envelope waiting for him. As he knew these would be the last words his father would ever share with him, he hesitated.

"You don't have to open it," Audrey whispered. "You could put it off until tonight or even next year. It is OK to save some things."

"I know," he replied, his eyes never leaving the envelope, "but I'm already three years late, so it needs to be done."

He peeled back the flap and retrieved the last note. After taking a deep breath, he read the words on the paper out loud.

"Jimmy, life is like a good cake, it takes certain ingredients to make it right. If you don't have just the right mix, you will always be disappointed in your life. Those ingredients don't come from inside you; they come from outside sources. They come from your friends and family; thus you must surround yourself with good people who bring good things into your life. You must read to find fresh ideas. I also think music is important. But the most important is faith, because without faith there is no hope.

"Think about the wise men when they brought their presents. They had never been to the place they were going and had never seen Jesus. Everything they did was on faith and hope. Thus, they understood faith and hope and how they work together. Jimmy, do you know what faith really is? It is believing in things you can't see, like the power of honesty, love, integrity, sacrifice, and trust. It is believing in yourself and your talents. Nothing of value can be seen until you have faith to believe. Faith is the most important thing in your life, and when you have that, people will put their hopes in you."

"But why the record player?" Audrey asked.

"There's more," Jimmy explained. "I think we're about to get to that."

Jimmy took a deep breath before continuing to read his father's words: "My son, you now have in your possession the final gift. The record on the turntable is my favorite Christmas song. It was written by a man who had lost his hope, but found it when he visited Bethlehem on Christmas Eve in 1865. I pray that each time you play this record you will feel the hope that brought light into the world on Christmas."

Jimmy set the letter to one side and studied the Victrola's arm. There was a needle. He grabbed the crank and wound it up; it worked. As the turntable spun, he placed the arm on the record. A rush of static was followed by a choir singing "O Little Town of Bethlehem." While the tone was not as sharp as it would have been on a new machine, the message was clear.

"A dead man speaks," Jimmy quietly said.

"Yes," she agreed. "And because of your dad, I actually listened to the words of that song. I'd never realized it was not as much about the birth of Jesus as it was about Jesus entering our hearts."

"The final spice," the boy whispered.

35

December 24, 1945, 9:16 p.m.

W hat a day," Jimmy said as he and his mother finished reading the Christmas story from Luke.

"Kind of nice we picked up the old traditions," she agreed. "I enjoyed watching you moving the pieces of the nativity scene around again as we went through the story. Brought back so many good memories. Though I'm still a bit confused as to why you left the wise men on the kitchen table."

Jimmy laughed. "They're not due for a while yet. I found that out earlier today."

"Who told you?" she asked.

Jimmy grinned. He hadn't informed her about his father's notes or gifts. He probably would down the road, but not yet. The time just wasn't right.

"And about this perfume," Marge scolded, "you didn't need to use your reward money for that."

"And you didn't need to buy me new clothes with your bonus either," he shot back.

"What a wonderful Christmas it has been," she sighed. "Did you know that Clark Miller gave me a big raise today? So you combine that with what you will be making next year and we can fix up a few things around here."

"Life is pretty sweet," he agreed.

"Only thing missing is your father," she sighed.

"No," Jimmy corrected her, "there is something else missing. We need the star on the top of the tree."

"Which one?" she asked.

The question hung in the air for a few moments as Jimmy considered the options. Yesterday, he would have chosen the glass star, but today he was a much different person. He had a greater understanding of life and his father. It was time not to resent the man's death, but to celebrate the way he had lived his life!

"Dad's medal needs to go up there," Jimmy said. "Hope often comes through sacrifice. As someone recently told me, we wouldn't celebrate Christmas unless there had been an Easter. Dad died the way he lived, and we need to be reminded of that!"

Marge nodded, wiped a tear from her cheek, set the Bible to one side, and stood. She crossed the room to the end table and pulled open the drawer. She reverently opened the box and carefully pulled out the Medal of Honor. Holding it by the ribbon, she studied it, more tears welling up in her eyes, before crossing over to the tree and draping the medal over the top branches.

"Perfect," Jimmy assured her.

She studied the new decoration for only a moment before quickly jerking her head back toward the door. Following her eyes, Jimmy got up and walked over to the window. "Looks like someone is coming up the driveway."

"Do you think it might be Audrey?" she teased. "I'm sensing sparks between you two."

"No," he answered, "she's at her grandmother's with her whole clan tonight."

Marge moved over beside him. "Then who could it be?"

"We'll know soon, Mom."

The car made the turn beside the barn and moved toward the house, its light beams bouncing off the snow-covered ground until it rolled to a stop. A few seconds later a door popped open and Calvin Jenkins emerged.

"Merry Christmas," he called out.

"Merry Christmas to you," Marge shouted back as she stepped out onto the porch. "What brings you out this time of night? Are you playing Santa Claus?"

As Jimmy joined his mother in the cold night air, the bus driver answered, "I'm substituting and I've a special delivery for you."

"Calvin," Marge said, "the candleholder was more than enough. It is beautiful."

Calvin didn't answer, instead he moved quickly to the other side of the car and opened the passenger door. He reached in and helped a figure out of the seat. It was too dark to make out his features, but the man was tall and terribly thin and carried a cane. After he emerged from the old Ford, he stood silently beside the car for a moment, his eyes focused on the porch.

Marge brought her hand to her mouth and whispered, "It can't be."

Jimmy glanced over at her. What was wrong? Why were tears pouring down her cheek?

He didn't have a chance to ask what was the matter before she literally raced down the steps and across the yard. A split second later she was throwing her arms around the visitor and sobbing like a child.

A confused Jimmy remained stock-still as the man dropped his cane and ran his fingers through Marge's hair. Finally, after more than a minute, she pulled back, and as she did, the man looked back at the house. "You've grown up, Son."

The voice was his father's—he was sure of that—but how was that possible? Kevin Buck had seen the cave blown to pieces. How could his father have survived that?

So a disbelieving Jimmy remained frozen as the man, his arm around Marge, moved across the yard. As the sixty-watt porch light hit his face, the boy finally had the proof he needed. Though he didn't understand how, his father had come home.

"Dad," he cried out as he rushed down the steps. "We were told you died—twice."

Wrapping his arms about the boy, Robert Reed whispered, "As Mark Twain once said, rumors of my demise have been greatly exaggerated. I guess I should have died, but the inside of the cave held up during the explosion, and there was a way out the back. It seems God always gave me an escape route that ultimately led back here."

As the two continued to hug, Marge whispered, "It's freezing out here. Let's get inside before someone catches a cold."

Robert stepped back from his son and said, "I see you haven't changed, Marge. Probably still harping on folks to button up before they go out."

"She sure does," Jimmy shot back, "but she is right—it is time to get inside."

As Jimmy and Marge helped Robert up the steps and into the house, Calvin got back in his car and drove off. He must have felt this night belonged to the Reeds and no one else.

Stopping at the front door, Robert paused and looked around. As he smiled, the age that had been apparent on his face a few seconds before seemed to evaporate. Suddenly he appeared not much different than his picture on the wall.

"It is so good to be home," he whispered.

As Marge helped Robert move farther into the room, Jimmy headed for the tree. Reaching up, he carefully pulled the medal from the branches and walked over to his father. "This is yours, Dad."

Jimmy raised the Medal of Honor over his father's head and lowered it until it rested on his shoulders. As Robert touched the medal for the first time, Jimmy noted the lighted candle in the wooden candleholder. The light was shining in such a way it illuminated the word *Hope.*

"I told you I'd come back," Robert assured his son. "I hope you never gave up on me."

"Only for a little while," Jimmy softly answered.

Discussion Questions

1. As the book opens, Jimmy is obviously angry. Who do you think he is angry with and can you justify his anger? How do you think you would feel if you were in his shoes?

2. Christmas has a much different meaning for Jimmy than it does for everyone else in town. Is Jimmy's attitude a reflection of his attitude toward God?

3. At first glance, Calvin does not appear to be wise man. Yet as the story evolves he seems to provide Jimmy with very simple lessons that hit home. Why is Calvin's life such a witness for others? What can you learn from the way he lives out his faith?

4. Why do you feel that Jimmy is joining a gang? Is he driven by his need for money? Is it an act of rebellion? Is it because he no longer believes in the merits of living by a moral code? Or is there something else that is pushing him?

5. Jimmy quickly realizes he has made a mistake by becoming a part of the gang. What events or people change his mind and why?

6. What role does Audrey play in the book? Do you think she is the mirror that shows Jimmy a reflection of himself he doesn't want to see, or does someone else act as that mirror?

7. In planning the heist, the gang uses the community's involvement in the church to ensure success. Why do you believe that churches held such a vital role in small communities during this era? Do they hold that role now? If not, why?

8. Although this is a book set at Christmas, the Scripture that seems to ring clearest with Jimmy as he looks at the meaning of living a Christian life is Matthew

25:35-40. After reading this Scripture how do you believe it ties in with the spirit of Christmas?

9. Jimmy's father sends him on the trail of three special gifts. How closely are each of these gifts tied to the gifts of the Magi? And why do you think Jimmy's father chose them as the means to teach important lessons for his son? If Jimmy had found them during the Christmas of 1942, do you believe he would have still joined the gang? Why or why not?

10. What is the real difference in hope and faith?

11. Jimmy changed a great deal from the first page in the book to the last. Do you believe that what he became was due to the way he had been raised or the lessons of those around him after he rebelled?

12. The star in this book was a Medal of Honor, but there are many stars used at Christmas. What star means the most to you and why?

Want to learn more about author
Ace Collins and check out other great fiction
from Abingdon Press?

Sign up for our fiction newsletter at
www.AbingdonPress.com
to read interviews with your favorite authors, find tips
for starting a reading group, and stay posted on what
new titles are on the horizon. It's a place to connect
with other fiction readers or post a
comment about this book.

Be sure to visit Ace online!

www.acecollins.com

What They're Saying About...

The Glory of Green, by Judy Christie
"Once again, Christie draws her readers into the town, the life, the humor and the drama in Green. *The Glory of Green* is a wonderful narrative of small-town America, pulling together in tragedy. A great read!"
—Ane Mulligan, editor of *Novel Journey*

Always the Baker, Never the Bride, by Sandra Bricker
"[It] had just the right touch of humor, and I loved the characters. Emma Rae is a character who will stay with me. Highly recommended!"
—Colleen Coble, author of *The Lightkeeper's Daughter* and the *Rock Harbor* series

Diagnosis Death, by Richard Mabry
"Realistic medical flavor graces a story rich with characters I loved and with enough twists and turns to keep the sleuth in me off-center. Keep 'em coming!"—Dr. Harry Krauss, author of *Salty Like Blood* and *The Six-Liter Club*

Sweet Baklava, by Debby Mayne
"A sweet romance, a feel-good ending, and a surprise cache of yummy Greek recipes at the book's end? I'm sold!"—**Trish Perry, author of** *Unforgettable* and *Tea for Two*

The Dead Saint, by Marilyn Brown Oden
"An intriguing story of international espionage with just the right amount of inspirational seasoning."—*Fresh Fiction*

Shrouded in Silence, by Robert L. Wise
"It's a story fraught with death, danger, and deception—of never knowing whom to trust, and with a twist of an ending I didn't see coming. Great read!"—Sharon Sala, author of *The Searcher's Trilogy: Blood Stains, Blood Ties,* and *Blood Trails*.

Delivered with Love, by Sherry Kyle
"Sherry Kyle has created an engaging story of forgiveness, sweet romance, and faith reawakened—and I looked forward to every page. A fun and charming debut!"—**Julie Carobini, author of** *A Shore Thing* and *Fade to Blue.*

Abingdon Press fiction
a novel approach to faith

AbingdonPress.com | 800.251.3320

Discover Fiction from Abingdon Press

BOOKLIST 2010

Top 10 Inspirational Fiction award

ROMANTIC TIMES 2010

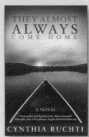

Reviewers Choice Awards
Book of the Year nominee

BLACK CHRISTIAN BOOK LIST

#1 for two consecutive months,
2010 Black Christian Book
national bestseller list;
ACFW Book of the Month, Nov/Dec 2010

CAROL AWARDS 2010

(ACFW) Contemporary
Fiction nominee

INSPY AWARD NOMINEES

Suspense   General Fiction   Contemporary Fiction

Abingdon Press fiction
a novel approach to faith
AbingdonPress.com | 800.251.3320